SOUTHSIDE KING

A Novel by

Alterick Gaston

Dedication

To Michael Anthony Atkinson

Preface

MEET THE PARENTS

Ms. Hattie Mae Jones was well known around Churchill as a booster and a con-woman. She was no more than 5'2", and she weighed about 125 pounds.

Although she was born and raised in poverty, she always seemed to carry herself like she was worth millions of dollars. She didn't keep her hair styled with extensions nor did she wear it braided.

Ever since she'd been a teen, she'd always been thick for her age. Now at the ripe age of 17, she had a figure that would put most of the women in the city of Richmond to shame, and she used what she had to get what she wanted. Like a lot of women in urban areas, she knew that men desired sex, and most were more than willing to pay for it.

Her mother, Mrs. Ada Mary Jones, was a whore who was killed by a serial killer known to the streets as, *The Black Pirate*, who would only attack the black, younger females. He was called the Black Pirate, because surviving victims of his attacks said he'd worn a black eye patch. She swore she would never go that route.

As Ms. Hattie Mae Jones was walking down the street, she heard a voice yell from across the street. "Hello, Chocolate Sundae!"

She ignored the comment and kept walking. The man quickly gave pursuit to catch up with her stride, as he called from behind her again. This time, she turned around.

She was about to curse him out but she recognized the handsome face of her first crush, who was also her first kiss, Ramon Baker.

He'd come a long way since the 5th grade, but shortly after, his family had moved away and she hadn't seen him since then.

5'4" had turned into a 6' even frame. The acne infested face now showed a smooth caramel-brown complexion, and basically, the only thing that appeared to have stayed the same was his big brown eyes; most women would refer to his eyes as *bedroom eyes*.

"Excuse me, but do I know you?" she asked, playing coy.

"Ain't you Hattie Mae?" he replied, breathing kind of hard from his effort to catch up to her.

"No, I don't think we've met before. Where do I know you from?" she asked without any emotion of excitement or real interest.

"Oh, you don't remember me, huh?" he stated, looking down on her sexy body.

"First off, if I did I wouldn't be asking who you are, now would I?" She snapped back. "Secondly, you can't answer a question with a question, can you?"

He looked stunned as if he'd heard that same line from somewhere before.

"You know Ms. McCall taught us better than that!" she said as she started laughing.

Relieved she'd actually remembered him, he joined her with his own laughter.

They spent the next few moments catching up on old times and each other. Ramon explained what had drawn him back to the capital of VA.

"My Uncle Jelly Bean is sick and needs me to handle the family business for a while."

"I'm sorry to hear that. Is he going to be alright?" Hattie asked sincerely. "He's always been such a nice man."

"Yeah, he's tough, but he just won't leave the underworld alone. I guess you also know he's been to prison twice, and he still loves fast money and even faster women," Ramon said followed by a chuckle. He's as tough as nails. He's been here this long, and I just have to believe he's not going nowhere no time soon," he added while wiping his forehead.

Hattie noticed the expensive Movado watch he had on, along with the time.

"I'm sorry Ramon, but I have to leave before I'm late for my appointment. I already missed my bus so I'll have to walk downtown and get to Woolworth's before closing."

"My fault, but I can give you a ride to make up for the lapse in time,' Ramon stated.

"I'd like that very much. Thank you, but as I recall you walked from behind me and I didn't see you drive up."

Ramon gave off a cocky laugh that only someone as assuring of his game could.

"Nah, Chocolate Sundae, you left out a part of the story. Before I walked or should I say ran you down, I had just gotten out of my car and was so stunned by your lovely face as well as your classy disposition, I left the engine running."

He smoothly pointed to the midnight blue '62 Cadillac at the corner of the block.

"I'm ready when you are. It shouldn't take us more than 10 minutes to hit Broad Street."

She hesitated at first then thought *fuck it!* She had to catch the store before closing time.

"Alright, but I'ma have to pay you 'cause I don't freeload off nobody!"

Ramon laughed again and stated, "Time is money. I held you up so I owe you for your time; it's the least I can do. No charge, this one is on me!"

He had a lot of game but she knew it would cost her, maybe a little, maybe a lot, but one thing was for sure, it would definitely cost.

As the radio played the latest hit, *My Girl*, by The Temptations. Ramon sang along with David Ruffin.

"*I got sunshine… on a cloudy day…when it's cold outside… I've got the month of May….*" Even though he was a debonair, he sounded like a drunken-wino around a fiery trash can in a back alley, but his efforts still made Hattie Mae blush.

As they pulled up in front of Woolworth's, Ramon turned the music down.

"Chocolate Sundae, would you do me the honor of joining me for dinner this evening?"

Hattie Mae started to decline but she had class, and most people in the hood knew not to pay to eat when you could eat for free.

"I'd like that very much, but you'll have to wait for me to finish my business here, due to the fact that it's a quarter 'til 5."

"No problem," Ramon replied, "I'll come in and wait for you."

"No!" Hattie Mae snapped. "Wait for me here. I'll be right out."

The last thing she wanted to do was let Ramon in on the fact that she was trying to run con on the young clerk at the Woolworth store. She also didn't want him to get caught up if the game went wrong. Fucking with white people's money in the South was more than dangerous, it was deadly.

Ramon looked at her as if he'd said something wrong.

"I was just trying to be a gentleman and escort you inside and make sure you returned safely."

"Naw, I'll be alright and my business won't take long. I just have to make a payment on my layaway," she said, running game on him, but she'd forgotten she couldn't play a playa.

"Lay-a-way?" Ramon asked. "Why pay a down-payment when you can buy the whole thing now...whatever it is?"

"Why you think, Ramon? I don't have the full amount right now. Or did you forget how it works in the *black* part of Richmond?"

Ramon laughed again, and his sinister laugh was starting to get on her nerves.

"I got you covered. How much you need?"

Hattie Mae was stunned but sharp enough to buy time as she thought of a digit that seemed reasonable.

"What? Nooo! I can't accept money from you, not for anything like this!"

Ramon played along. "It's nothin', fo'real. What you need, $25, $50, $75, or $100?"

Not wanting to turn down some quick money but not wanting to appear greedy, she replied, "$50 should cover it."

"Ok," Ramon stated, "But I'm comin' in with you."

Hattie Mae had played herself out of pocket, but it was no use on debating and time was of the essence.

"Alright, but give me the $50 now, because I don't want these white folk to think I'm a whore or something."

Ramon shot back, "Fuck them crackers! As far as they know, we're married."

Hattie Mae then responded, "Where's my ring, then?"

She had a point but Ramon always had to have the last word. Reaching inside his pocket for his bill fold he then replied, "Consider me the pawn shop, and along with the fine China our people also gave us a *monetary* wedding gift," he said with a smirk on his face. They both laughed as he handed her the $50 dollar bill and they exited the car.

Hattie Mae slipped the $50 inside her purse and removed a $5 dollar bill. As they walked inside the store, she needed to somehow get Ramon away from her.

"Babe, I need you to get something for me while I handle this business."

Ramon was pleased she'd finally recognized him as a man and let him take charge and do something nice for her.

'Anything for you my Chocolate Sundae," he replied.

"Anything babe?" she asked.

"Anything," he said licking his lips.

Her panties instantly got wet from the thought of his lips touching her, and not the ones that could speak words either.

"I need some feminine napkins."

Ramon hadn't been prepared for that, and he was completely caught off guard. "Feminine what?" he repeated her request.

"My fault, I meant some maxi pads," she said bluntly, "They're back there on the personal hygiene aisle."

The young white woman behind the counter laughed under her breath, as she looked down at the newspaper pretending not to be listening and watching them.

Ramon began pointing down the aisle, "This way?" he asked Hattie Mae.

"Yes, you'll see them. You *do* know what they look like, right?"

He shot her a look and began walking to the back to retrieve the maxi pads she'd asked for.

Hattie gathered herself and approached the counter. As she approached, the woman behind the counter gave her a smile and asked, "How can I help you?" Hattie shot her back with her best smile and said and answered, "I'd like to see your catalog and get my vase out of layaway."

The clerk wondered how a black woman could even get a layaway plan here at Woolworths.

"Excuse me. Did you say layaway?" The clerk asked pretending not to have believed her ears.

"Yes, here's the slip," she stated, answering her next question before the woman could even ask.

The slip was from the store, alright. How could it not be when she had stolen it from the old white lady she'd met at City Hall earlier that day, while in a bathroom stall?

"Your balance is $25.00," the clerk said, "How much do you plan on putting down on this vase today?"

"I plan to pay the complete balance," Hattie stated with a smirk. For some reason, it seemed to be taking much longer to complete the transaction than she imagined. She was trying to take care of this matter before Ramon could return from the back of the store.

As the clerk researched the log book, Hattie removed the $50 dollar bill from her purse.

"Here we are Ms. Robinson," the clerk said, while eyeing the $50 dollar bill she had removed from her purse. She then picked up the phone and gave the person on the other end some information before hanging up. She shot Hattie a phony smile.

Hattie didn't seem to mind her racial indifferences, because she was about to make her pay.

"Your vase is on its way. Would you like to have it gift wrapped?" the clerk asked, trying to play nice.

"No thank you ma'am."

"Here you go, Chocolate Sundae!" She heard a familiar voice say, as Ramon placed the napkins on the counter.

The clerk noticed how big Ramon's hands were, as he placed the box on the counter. Even though she had never committed the taboo act considered to be an unlawful sin of sleeping with a black man, she recalled the many stories she'd heard about them having big members.

"Thank you sweetheart," Hattie said.

The clerk looked up at Ramon and smiled, and Hattie caught it; the clerk was clearly attracted to Ramon.

This two-faced bitch, Hattie thought, she got some nerve eying my man, knowin' damn well she could have Ramon jailed for reckless eye-ballin' or even worse.

"Here's the vase you ordered Ms. Robinson," the young white boy said.

"Thank you young man," Hattie replied.

"Jane, Uncle Bill said he'll give you a ride home if you like and y'all can go by lover's lane after he drops me off."

The young boy had caught Jane by surprise with his remarks and she blushed out from embarrassment.

"John boy, you're too grown for your age, and furthermore, I have no idea what you're talking about! Why did you bring this merchandise up here anyway?" the woman asked hoping the boy would leave.

She was trying to kill two birds with one stone by making her seem like a class act in front of Ramon and wanting to change the topic, as she removed her blonde hair from her left eye with her left hand, revealing a one-karat, marquise diamond and gold engagement ring.

Cold freak! Was the thought that ran across both Ramon's and Hattie Mae's mind.

"He spilled coffee all over his shirt while trying to get the vase out of storage."

That's Bill for ya', Jane thought. If his daddy wasn't William Woolworth and he wasn't heir to the throne, she would've rejected his proposal of marriage. Other than her looks, she was poor, white trash, so having finances before romance was a must.

"Oh yeah Ms. Robinson, Bill said to make sure your brother Bob picks him up Sunday and not Saturday, so they can go fishing."

Hattie didn't respond. She was stuck, and Ramon caught on. "I'll tell him, thank you John Boy," she finally replied. There was a stunned silence for a split second.

"Okay, I'm gone to the back. It was nice meeting y'all," John Boy said, as he grabbed a candy bar off the shelf.

Ramon quickly turned his attention to the clerk. "The man who put that ring on your finger sure is lucky," he said in a flirtatious manner.

"You think so, huh?" Jane smiled looking back at him.

"You're a very beautiful woman, and you'd make any man proud to call you his *wife*," Ramon said, stressing the word any, as he placed his left hand on the counter, revealing a diamond encrusted, initial, pinky ring with the letters R.B.

Jane smelled money and romance. She was drawn in by him agreeing to get the feminine napkins for his lady friend, something Bill would've never done. The man who stood before her was fine and not broke. The only problem was his race, which overruled the positives.

"Can we handle this so we can go?" Hattie interrupted.

But the eye contact between the two was unbreakable. Jane rang up the cash register and said "$25.00 even please."

Ramon had seen the $5.00 dollar bill in Hattie's hand as she handed it over to Jane and said, "Look here Ms...."

Jane cut him off and added, "Nixon, Jane Nixon."

"Well Ms. Nixon, my name is Everett Bains. I'm in town for a few days on business from NYC, and I see you have some nice items in this store. I'd like to come back and purchase something beautiful for a nice lady who works very hard and deserves it," he said winking his eye, "So, do you think you can help me out?"

"Sure," Jane replied, "But there are lots of stores around, with better stuff than what you see here."

"Such as?" Ramon asked.

"Such as, Thalheimers, Macy's, Fine Fur factory and Megan's Jewelry, those are the places a female loves to receive gifts from," Jane said with the intention of dropping a hint.

"Hopefully, while I'm here, you can find the time to show me these stores and help me do some shopping for a special friend I met today.

"Ms. Robinson is a Richmond native. I'm sure she can show you around and help you pick up something of her liking," Jane said.

"Who said it was for Ms. Robinson? How do you know it's not you I'm referring to?"

Jane was stuck by the question, and Hattie was upset that Ramon had the nerve to even make a bold statement yet she had to seize the moment.

"I'd like to pay for this now," Hattie added.

"Jane was so caught off guard, and in lust with the black Don Juan, she hadn't even bothered to look at the $5.00 dollar bill Hattie had slipped her. She had never taken her eyes off of Ramon.

"My change please," Hattie stated, with an out-stretched palm.

"Yes, of course," Jane said, as she began to reach back into the register for a $20 dollar bill and the same $5 dollar bill Hattie had just given her.

"Bag please," Hattie stated again.

"I'm sorry," Jane managed to say while breaking the trance-like stare she had fixated on Ramon.

"Here you are." She quickly bagged the vase, handed Hattie the receipt and the deal was sealed.

"Thank you. Ernest we'll be going now."

"Right after you," Ramon said, not breaking eye contact with Jane.

As they walked off towards the door, Jane noticed something was wrong and she couldn't put her finger on it right away, but the answer was right in front of her face.

"Hey, wait a minute!" Jane screamed as Hattie's hand was on the exit door. "Come back here!"

Ramon told Hattie to wait in the car as he went back over to the counter. "If I'm not back in 5 minutes...leave!" he said to Hattie.

Hattie looked as if she was about to lose it, as she nodded her understanding to Ramon. She headed for the car feeling bad for even letting Ramon drop her off. If she had just left, everything would've gone smooth. As she turned back to look at Ramon approaching the counter, she noticed the register was still open.

"Look at this shit here," she said under her breath, as she crossed the street headed for the car.

Ramon approached the counter. "Yes, is there a problem?" he asked.

"You forgot your lady friend's napkins!"

Ramon was relieved to know she hadn't penned the game. He smiled and replied, "No, actually I forgot two things."

Looking puzzled, Jane wondered what it could be. Reading her facial expression, he said..."I forgot the napkins and I also forgot to get your phone number."

Jane smiled quickly, bagged the napkins up, and wrote her phone number down on the bag.

"What's a good time to call?" he asked.

"Late tonight, after 10pm," Jane said while looking towards the back of the store.

"No problem," Ramon replied. He slipped her $5 dollars and said, "Keep the change." The napkins were only 75 cents, and he wanted to show Jane he was paid and spending it was nothing.

Exiting the store, he turned back to catch one last look at Jane, and licked his lips. "After 10 tonight, right," he said with a wink. She just nodded her head, and there was nothing else to say; the deal was sealed.

Hattie had tears forming in her eyes as she saw Ramon exiting the store. She was on the verge of crying out of fear for him, but now it was excitement to know they'd gotten away, still, she wondered what Ramon had said with his slick talking ass. Then it hit her, Jane called him back to flirt with him. *Just like them ole men! Stealin' white heifers, it ain't enough they got all the money and nice houses in Richmond, but they want the good black men, too! Fuck that! Not this time and Ramon with his slick fine ass…. flirtin' with her right in front of me like I wasn't even there? Wait 'til his ass get in this car. I got something to tell his ass,* she thought to herself, getting angrier by the second.

"That was close," Ramon stated as he opened up the car door.

"The only thing that was close was your fresh ass and that fast heifer!" Hattie snapped.

"What the hell are you talkin' 'bout?" Ramon shot back as he started up the car.

Hattie's voice was immediately drowned out by the sounds of the radio. Smokey Robinson and the Miracles started singing to their ears.

"My Mama told me……. you better shop around…"

Hattie turned down the volume, as Ramon pulled away from the curb. "You either got a lot of nerve or you're a heartless muthafucka!" she shot at Ramon. *Ernest Bains,* the white-lady-lover! It's dudes like you that make women like me, hate ghetto-hustling black men. Give me a square any day! At least they wouldn't dream of looking at a white woman the way you looked at that bitch, carrying on and what not! They already know…"

Ramon cut her off. "Know what? How to kiss a cracker's ass for chump change? Shit, they might as well still be in slavery. They don't own shit, 'cause whatever they're makin' payments on belongs to the white man. So, they work for a white man to make money, then turn around and give it back to the white man to pay their bills. And for those that call themselves lucky enough to *own* something, they have to pay taxes on shit to the white man! So don't call him a square! Call him a slave!"

Hattie had never looked at it like that.

"Furthermore...," Ramon continued, "If I hadn't been there to slick talk her ass, you would've gotten popped!"

The words struck a nerve in Hattie. "What the hell you mean *popped*? Over a layaway slip and this funky ass $200 vase? Boy, please, I been runnin..."

"Runnin what?" Ramon kept going, "That bullshit ass note game that played out with the zoot suit?"

Hattie had no idea he'd seen it. She made a mental note to work on her exchange. "You saw that, huh?" she said in a lower voice, more ashamed that she'd been caught by him and not by the clerk at the store.

"How could I not? The shit was as slow as cold molasses," Ramon jokingly said, "But Chocolate Sundae, don't worry, from here on out, I got you!"

"What do you mean by that?" Hattie asked.

"I got you from here on out. I'll take care of you," Ramon answered.

"I understand that part," Hattie stated with a firmness to let him know she wasn't hard of hearing.

"What part don't you understand then?" Ramon asked.

"Why do you keep callin' me Chocolate Sundae?" She was looking straight into his eyes to see if he was speaking from his heart.

Ramon pulled the car over at the curb on Marshall Street at the corner of 23rd street.

He then looked her in her eyes and replied,

"Listen, if I offended you by that, I'm sorry. It's not like Hattie isn't a beautiful name, it's just that it's my Grandma's name; she passed away when I was 13 years old....God rest her soul. I just don't want to call my wife by that name. It hurts too much. Chocolate Sundae fits you just fine in my eyes." He began rubbing her face with the back of his hand. "You have the softest, milk chocolate skin, and your pecan-brown eyes are a bonus. You look delectable to the eye. The chocolaty topping is only the outer shell. The true delight comes from the sweetness within, and even though I have yet to taste you, you'll always be my favorite desert.

Hattie began to speak but only to be silenced by his forefinger crossing her lips.

"My Grandma Hattie always gave me Chocolate Sundaes when I was a good boy. I guess I've been good, because when I saw you and remembered your name, it was a sign from Grandma showing me I need to be here for her only boy, Jelly Bean."

Hattie now had tears in her eyes, as she felt a feeling she'd never felt before. As a little girl, her mother Ada had always told her when a good man always held his mother and grandmother in high regard, he'd hold his wife in high regard just the same.

"So, as you can see, this is bigger than some con-game or anything else in this life thus far," Ramon said, with a sense of firmness that assured her he wasn't playing any games.

"So, where do we go from here?" Hattie asked.

"To the top of the world and anywhere else you wanna go," he answered.

"Well, I wanna go to the pawn shop on 25th street right now," Hattie said with a smile on her face.

"And while we're there, we can get you a ring and make this thing official," Ramon added in, and from that day forward, the two were inseparable.

It had only been a few months since Hattie had moved in with Ramon, at one of Jelly Bean's houses in the Blackwell area in South Richmond. She didn't have to work or hustle; she was a simple housewife whose only job was to concentrate on the home.

She'd just found out she was pregnant with their first child, and she couldn't wait to tell Ramon because she knew how he had longed to have his own children.

As soon as he'd come through the door, she could sense something was wrong.

"Babe, I have some bad news," he said, with his eyes full of sadness and tears.

"What's wrong?" Hattie asked, showing nothing but the genuine love and concern a wife should.

"Jelly is dead," Ramon said with a crack in his tone, as the lumps began swelling in his throat.

"What! How?" Hattie asked, while reaching for her man to comfort him, as he let all his cries of hurt and pain finally come out.

They embraced one another and shared a grieving moment. Ramon then explained how Jelly had a heart attack while having sex with the young girl Boochie, who had just moved there from North Carolina, to attend school at Virginia Union University. *Well, Jelly Bean had always said, one of them young girls gonna be the death of me,* Ramon thought to himself, as a small smile spread across his face at the memory and irony of it all.

Hattie knew if anything ever happened to Jelly Bean their lives would drastically change, mainly because everything would fall on Ramon.

Jelly's funeral was the most lavish the city of Richmond had ever seen. All the major players of the city came out in full attire. There were so many fur coats from sables, minks, foxes, and rabbits. One might wonder if there were any animals left to keep the zoos open.

Jelly had on a custom made, cream colored, Brook's Brothers Suit and a blood-red neck tie. His casket was solid oak and trimmed in 14 karat gold. He was being put away beautifully.

All the women in the Urban Area were there, most to pay their respects, others to try and catch a major player from the underworld. Overall, it was a lovely service.

To Hattie's surprise, number running was only part of the illicit activities Jelly Bean had left for Ramon to rule. He was also involved in the heroin trade, along with numerous after hour spots and whore houses. All of which directly affected her family but for how long? Only time would tell...

Keeping Traditions

As the saying went, *when one family member died, another was born.* In Hattie's and Ramon Baker's case...six more were born.

Their first born was a boy named Thomas, after Ramon's Grandfather the boot-legger. Raymond was the second oldest, named after Hattie's Grandfather. The third son was Ramon, Jr. and the fourth was Tousant to honor Jelly Bean. The fifth son was named Hank and the sixth and final child was Sandra, a girl.

Hattie and Ramon promised once they had a little baby girl, their baby making days would be over.

At Hattie's request, they never left the house that Jelly Bean had given them over in the Blackwell area. That's where they had laid their roots.

Despite having Ramon Sr. to provide for her and their children, Hattie hated the dirty money. Numbers and liquor was one thing, but whores and drugs were something totally different. Besides, she was a hustler; it was in her blood.

During the summer months when school was out, she noticed how the children in the neighborhood ran around late nights. The corner store would close up early, where they all hung out, when they weren't swimming or doing some childhood mischief.

One day, she was struck with a new idea, and she started selling candy, cookies, sodas and other snacks to the kids in the neighborhood, that way she could keep her own children closer to home.

With Ramon backing her, she became Richmond's first candy lady. Others would soon follow suit but she was the first to sell everything the corner store had, except for alcoholic beverages. She instead made ice-burgs in the summer time. It was a frozen mix of sugar, Kool-Aid, and water.

Hattie set a tone that would soon be copied in every neighborhood around Richmond. Ramon loved Hattie and his children dearly, but like most street hustlers, he had a strong jones in his bones for sleeping with different women. Although he didn't have any other children out of wedlock, he had plenty of women.

Jane Woolworth was his cash cow. When Bill had mysteriously drowned in a boating accident, Ramon had access to all the money he needed, until she realized he was never going to leave his family so they could be together the way she'd dreamed they would be.

However, by that time, Ramon, Sr. had amassed a fortune in real estate. It was the hustler's greed that he'd remain in the street life. Although his children had the very best life had to offer, the vibe of the hustle was deeply rooted in their veins. As the streets talked, they listened and they soon realized, their parents were the only role models they'd ever need or want.

Chapter 1

Ramon and Jane had just left the Jefferson Hotel together, after a night of passionate love making.

"Babe, you know we're takin' a big risk by bein' seen in public," Jane explained to Ramon, as they approached her pink '57 Cadillac.

"It really doesn't matter now. It's not like it's still against the law or something," Ramon said frankly, "Besides, we're just very good friends," he added, winking his eye at her.

They made their way to the car, and Ramon removed the keys and popped the trunk. As he began to reach inside, two police cruisers pulled into the parking lot, jumped out, and pulled their pistols.

"Freeze nigger!" Officer Carter yelled out. "Thank God, you're here!" Jane screamed as she ran from Ramon's side.

I can't believe this bitch! Ramon thought to himself furious, she just sucked my dick dry, drinkin' all my future children and then let me fuck her up the ass, while saying how much she loved me! And now she's running to the police, knowing I got half a key in the trunk?"

"Put your hands in the air and slowly turn around, nigger boy!" Officer Don Carter commanded.

Ramon turned to face the officers, as he witnessed Jane crying fake tears. While looking into his eyes she smiled and mouthed the words, "Payback's a bitch." She was thinking to herself, *if I can't have my black dick to myself then no one else will have it either. Think he's gonna fuck me then return home to his family like everything is fine. I'd rather send him to jail, make him sign the divorce papers, and then marry him before he's released. Afterwards, I'll pay the commonwealth's attorney to drop the charges.*

Ramon wasn't going to prison for no shit like this. It would cost him too much and hurt his family dearly. He had to remain calm and think of a way out of the situation.

"Okay, y'all just be cool; I ain't gone put up no fight," Ramon said, as he looked for a direction to take off running.

"On the ground nigger!" the other officer Mark Oversheet said, "We been waitin' for the day we could finally bust Ramon Baker. No jury would be bought for trying to rape and kidnap a white woman; not just any white woman but Jane

Woolworth Co-CEO of Woolworth's store," the officer added in, with a devious smirk across his face.

As Ramon began to lower himself to the ground, he noticed a look in Officer Carter's eyes, and it was deeper than hatred; it was pure evil as if the devil himself was approaching with a cocked gun.

Every bone in Ramon's body told him if he didn't run or get Jane to change her story, he'd be a dead man. Since the ladder of the two seemed impossible, he got down in a four-point stance, repeating loudly, "Don't shoot!"

As soon as his hands touched the ground, he took off like Jessie Owens, headed in the opposite direction of the squad cars.

POP! POP!

The first two shots missed Ramon. As he turned the corner, he could here Jane screaming, "Don't kill him!" He was running for his life.

"Don, where you going?" officer Chestnut yelled to no avail.

Don Carter had already made his mind up that Ramon Baker wasn't getting away. As Officer Carter turned the corner, he had a clear shot at Ramon's back.

POP! POP! The gun sounded off with a thunderous clap.

Ramon felt a sharp pain in his back. He tried to continue moving, but the message his brain tried to send to his legs never seemed to make it. The fire in between his back and his chest felt like someone had lit a book of matches and put them inside of his body. He found it hard to breath, as his knees buckled beneath him.

Slowly, he'd fallen face-first onto the cold concrete. *Crack*, the pain shot up from his mouth to his eye, and then to his head. Blood shot out from his mouth, along with his two, front, gold teeth.

He watched the sun sparkle a blinding light off his bloody covered teeth. Suddenly, he saw his Uncle Jelly Bean waving at him.

"Over here babe boy, it's a lot safer over here," he heard Uncle Jelly Bean say.

Ramon suddenly felt the strength to get up and run, but for some reason, he didn't want to move. He blinked and saw Officer Carter putting a gun in his right hand. Ramon tried to pull the gun up and pull the trigger, but he had no strength. He heard Jane sobbing and screaming, as she ran toward him, reaching down to his limp body.

"Breathe babe, breathe!" Ramon heard Jane say. He tried, but instead of air, only blood shot out. "Breathe damn it breathe!" she yelled again.

"Call for help you bastards!" Jane yelled at the police.

"Hold on babe, hold on!" She instructed Ramon.

Finally Ramon tried to speak, but he couldn't. He again saw his Uncle Jelly Bean and reached for his hand. Jelly Bean smiled, reaching out his hand to Ramon saying, "Let it go." and just like that, Ramon let out his final breath. His hand fell limp before Jane had a chance to grab it, and now it seemed as though she'd gotten her wish after all. She couldn't have Ramon Baker and now, no other woman could either.

Chapter 2

"Amazing grace...how sweet...the sound..." the choir of First Baptist church sang over the body of Ramon Baker Sr. Although, Ramon Jr. was the third child, he acted as if he were the oldest.

He sat next to his mother Hattie on the front row, as thoughts began flooding his mind

"My daddy is dead behind that trifling, white, piece-of-shit whore. Them pussy ass police are gonna pay for this one day, when the time is right, I'ma do 'em all in!"

"Vengeance is mine said the Lord," Pastor Atkinson said, as if he were talking directly to Ramon, Jr. "The Lord giveth and the Lord taketh away."

The Pastor continued to talk beautifully about Ramon, Sr. as low sobs could be heard everywhere around the church. Hattie wouldn't cry, as she rocked in Ramon Jr.'s arms during the whole sermon.

Ramon was buried in the same manner as Jelly Bean, except his casket was solid black oak, with gold trimming, and a picture of a black Jesus with open arms, looking down over his body crying.

"Ramon," Sandra whispered to him from his left side, "That's not daddy up there."

With Sandra being the only girl, she'd taken things to her father the most out of any of the other children, and she was always the closest to Ramon.

"Daddy's still here with us. That's not him in that casket, that's just a shell of what we thought was him. His soul is with God, but his spirit is with us always."

"Especially in you Ramon," Hattie spoke. It was the first time in days she'd said anything. I'm ready to go now and get this over with." With that, she stood up, and Pastor Atkinson stopped his sermon.

Hattie approached the altar where Ramon's casket rest. She bent down, kissed his forehead softly and said, "Babe, I love you, and I pray you can rest now. God took you for a reason. His Will, I will never question. I'll see you again soon, sweetheart. I love you forever."

Turning to face a silent church she cleared her throat and said, "Thank you all for coming out. We really appreciate all of those who are here to support us in our time of need, but there are some fake people amongst us as well."

Hattie looked to the back of the church directly into the face of Jane Woolworth. If they hadn't been in the Lord's house she would've given her a piece of her mind. If it hadn't been for the police escort, she would've made sure they put her body under her husband's casket, since she desired for Ramon Sr. to be on top of her so much.

"I'm not going to judge, because God knows whose heart is pure." Pastor Atkinson, thank you for your prayers and support, and the rest of the church, as well. I'm ready to leave now. My husband is with God and he's not coming back. Mr. Mimms, you and your sons can grant my husband's final wishes after our children give their final goodbyes."

She returned to the front row and instructed her children to make their peace.

Thomas was the first to get up and approach his father's coffin. "Daddy, I'm gone miss you and thank you for everything. We gone take care of each other and look after Mama."

Tousant was next. "Daddy I'm gone finish school like you always wanted me to, and I promise to make you proud. We live to die, but you're always with us."

Ramon was next, but he bent down and whispered so no one else in the church could hear him. "I will avenge you and make you proud. "As he looked up toward the sky with tears running down his face, he whispered his final plea, "God, please take care of my daddy."

Ray was next to go. "Daddy I love you and I'm gone miss you." Trying hard to hide his emotion, he was really never one for a lot of words.

"Daddy I love you, and we gone remain as strong as we always do R.I.P. pops," Hank said.

Sandra was the one to approach her father's casket. Ramon held her up as she took baby steps, on wobbly legs. As soon as she'd made it close enough, she tried to jump in, as she began shouting from the depth of her soul, "Take me with you daddy! I gotta go with you!" she screamed out, as Ramon, Hank, and Ray pulled her back.

The entire church seemed to break down into tears, as they watched his daughter's heart-break. Some cried aloud, others cried silently. Sandra fought hard to get away from her brothers but to no avail. Finally, she fainted.

Hank, Thomas, and Ray carried her out of the church. Ramon approached his mother as she got up from her seat.

Hattie spoke directly to Mr. Mimms, "If there is anyone here who wants to view my husband's body, let them look as they pass now. No pictures, just one last look before you grant him his final wish. There will be no concession of cars, just take him to our family plot on Maury Street. I'll know where to find him."

Hattie and Ramon proceeded to walk out of the church. As they got near the exit where Jane and some officers were standing, Ramon felt rage the in his body boiling.

Hattie stopped right in front of Jane, and the two officers stepped up, as Jane simultaneously jumped back. Ramon quickly pulled his mother out of harm's way of the police, while other people at the service brace themselves behind him. It was about to go down, but Hattie suddenly stepped in and intervened.

"No! Not today or any day! The Lord will take care of my revenge," she stated, looking Jane dead in her eyes.

Ramon was less forgiving, and he spat on one of the officers' badges." You cowards have no business dwelling in the house of our Lord," he said coldly.

"Mr. Mimms," Hattie shouted from the exit, "You can proceed now."

Following her instructions, they opened the bottom half of the opened casket and turned Ramon's body over onto his stomach.

He always did like to have the last word, Hattie thought, as she exited the church with the beloved Ramon, joining the rest of the family, waiting outside in the car.

Chapter 3

It had been a few weeks since the funeral of Ramon Baker, Sr. and things had changed drastically. A lot of money in the streets remained in the streets. All the real estate, besides their house on 12th St., where they lived now, belonged to Jane Woolworth. They were essentially broke.

"Ramon, we got to do something if we don't come up with a plan, everything daddy worked so hard for is gonna crumble," Thomas said, words slurring, while drinking a bottle of Night Train.

"Never that," Ramon said, "My word is my bond. We gonna get all that's owed to us, one way or another, all debts will be paid."

"I'm with you bruh," Tousant said, "Whatever it takes."

Ramon and Thomas looked at each other, and then looked at Tousant.

"You goin' to school, and you gonna get your education like daddy always wanted you to," Thomas said rather bluntly.

"I'll take care of everything else," Ramon added. Y'all just be cool." It was the coldness in his voice that let them know he was dead serious.

The three of them sat quietly in the living room of the family's house. The silence was broken minutes later by a knock on the door.

"Who is it?" Ramon asked with a lot of bass in his voice.

"Fat Man!" said the voice.

"Hold up shawty!" Ramon replied, with a hint of excitement.

He and Fat Man had been friends for years. They were as close as brothers, and many people on the street thought they actually were. Ramon opened the door and gave him some dap followed by a brotherly hug.

"My main man, Ramon, come on shawty, let's ride." Fat Man said.

"Let me grab my coat," Ramon said, as he headed for the closet.

Fat Man stepped inside and pulled the door so he wouldn't let the heat out.

"What's up fellas?" Fat Man said to Thomas and Tousant.

"Chillin," they both responded simulataneously.

"I'll holla at y'all," Fat Man said as he exited the house.

"Later," Tousant and Thomas said.

Fat Man had left the engine running on the black '72 Lincoln. As soon as they pulled away from the curb, he turned the music down.

"Look here bruh," he said not taking his eyes off the road, "Shit is wicked out here. Mufuckas ain't got no loyalty, wouldn't none of these bitch-ass-niggas be eatin' if your pops ain't feed 'em."

"I know. It's like mufuckas forgot where they came from," Ramon added. "Did you get what I asked you for?"

"Fo' sho," Fat Man answered.

"Where you think we goin'?"

Ramon just smiled as he thought of how things would soon unfold.

The Lincoln turned on Hull Street and headed uptown to Ronnie and Connie Richardson's house.

Fat Man and Ramon had met the girls in high school their junior year at J.H.W. High. Fascinated by the legend of Ramon Baker's mystic, they found Ramon Baker, Jr., irresistible. Ramon and Fat Man preyed and thrived off the allure of these types of females.

As they pulled up to the house on 33rd street, the sisters were on the front porch smoking a jay and holding two duffel bags.

"'Bout time these niggas brought they ass 'round here. Got us waitin' out here like some ole rundown hoes," Ronnie said as they both reached down to get the bags.

"Shit, after this lick we ain't gone have to fuck with none of these lame niggas again, watch!" Connie said.

Connie was younger than Ronnie by a year, but she always presented herself as one of those *know-it-all* types of female.

Ramon watched them as they walked towards the car.

"You think these bitches ready for this?" he asked Fat Man.

"If they wasn't they wouldn't be headed towards the car," Fat Man stated frankly.

Ramon knew Fat Man was right but there was no room for error.

"Hey boo," Ronnie said, knowing she had fucked both of the gangstas."

"What's up?" Fat Man replied with a serious tone.

"Y'all ready?" Ramon asked.

"Damn you don't say hi, kiss my ass or nothing!" Connie snapped. She had just fucked Ramon two weeks ago, and like most young girls, she felt like fucking him had made her a part of his world.

"It ain't like that," Ramon said, only because he needed them, but in his mind he could care less if the young girl got hit by a truck. I just got something on my mind," Ramon said, telling a half-truth, which was only half way better than a lie.

"Oh I thought so," Connie replied in a joking manner. Don't worry, boo. Don't I always take care of you?" she added, as if she and Ramon had been an item for years; at least in her mind they were.

"This is some serious shit. You know what it can lead to right?" Fat Man said as he pulled from the curb, headed towards Midlothian turnpike.

"Y'all just hold on to y'all end of the deal and we'll handle our business," Ronnie said, knowing she had to take charge before Connie fucked it up for the both them.

They turned up in Jefferson Village Apts., one of the deadliest areas in Richmond, VA. They pulled into the back and parked in the parking lot. All four of them got out and headed towards the last apartment building.

Entering the hallway, they let the girls go first as they pulled their guns from their jackets, cocked and loaded and ready to pop off. No one was in the hallway, as Ronnie scanned her surroundings before knocking on the door.

"Felicia, open the door with your crazy ass!" Connie yelled loud enough so everybody inside the building could hear her, especially the people in the apartment who had their music blasting through the paper thin walls.

"Hold up!" Felicia answered back with attitude. She really hated to be interrupted while getting her groove on. Her baby's daddy, Stank, was in town and she had to have some dick before he went back to his current girlfriend CeeCee.

Ronnie and Connie were her girls from way back, and besides that, they were there to buy some food stamps.

"Girl you know y'all early and shit," she continued as she opened the door with nothing but a house coat on. She was greeted by the barrel of a .357 as her hands went straight in the air.

"Don't make a sound bitch!" Ramon said as he entered the house.

Felicia backed up, her house coat fully open exposing her naked body. Her breasts were big and ripe and stood full with erect nipples. The only flaw on her carmel complexion, were the stretch marks on her breasts and stomach, along with a scar from a past C section she'd undergone.

"Take what you want, just don't hurt me!" Felicia said. As fear overtook her, she began shaking uncontrollably.

"Where he at!" Ramon asked.

Felicia pointed to the back room.

"Who else here?" Ramon probed further.

"Just the baby, Lord, please don't hurt my baby," Felicia pleaded, dropping to her knees.

Ronnie and Connie came through the door with the bags, and Fat Man had his gun to both of their backs.

"Babe, hurry up! You know we on borrowed time," Stank yelled from the back.

Ramon headed straight for the back room.

"Girl, just do what they say and we'll be alright," Connie said.

"Bitch shut up and get on the couch," Fat Man said, pointing his gun directly in Connie's face.

Not knowing if he was for real or not, Connie and Ronnie both dropped their bags and helped Felicia off the floor.

"'Bout time shit! I was startin' to think..." Stank was cut off by the sight of Ramon's gun aimed squarely between his eyes, as Stank had truly been caught with his drawers down.

"You know what time it is nigga!" Ramon said, walking towards the bed.

Stank tried to buy himself some time, "Hold up shawty, don't shoot, I ain't got shit," he pleaded, knowing he was lying.

Ramon slapped him square across the bridge of his nose with the butt of the gun. Blood shot across the room and up on the ceiling, as the sound of a breaking bone echoed throughout the room.

"Oh shit!" Stank said, grabbing his face, "Damn man, you broke my shit! Oh man, you muthafucka," Stank continued as the blood gushed through his fingers and all over the bed, as he bounced around in pain. The sight gave Ramon an instant head-rush. The power of complete control, over life or death, really boosted his ego.

"Shut up pussy and stop crying like a bitch! You either give it to me or you give it to God, your choice!" Ramon said, pressing the barrel of the gun against Stank's left temple.

"It's in the car! The keys are on the dresser! Just don't kill me and my family, man. Let my son and my girl go, they ain't got shit to do with this," Stank pleaded in desperation.

"Get your ass out of the bed nigga!" Ramon demanded.

Stank went to reach for his pants on the floor.

"Try something stupid and all of y'all gone die today, nigga! Now, I said……..get your ass out of bed now!" Ramon replied again taking no chances.

Stank got out of the bed, butter-ball-naked, holding his bloody face as he walked out of the room. *If I live all these motherfuckers gone die,* Stank thought, as the feeling in his face went numb.

As soon as he entered the living room, he saw Felicia, Ronnie and Connie hog tied and duct taped. Fat Man held his baby boy in his arms, with the gun aimed directly in the baby's chest.

Stank felt helpless, but understood, giving full cooperation was the only way everyone would come out of this alive.

"Get your bitch ass on the floor," Ramon said, kicking Stank in the back of one knee. Catching him off balance, Stank hit the floor like a sack of potatoes.

"Just take what you came for and go," Stank pleaded again.

"Where the list at?" Fat Man asked.

"What list?" Stank asked looking at Felicia. He could see the fear in her eyes, and it was clear she'd been traumatized by the current chain of events.

"Shawty, do ya' girl and baby a favor, tell the truth or else!" Ramon said coldly.

Stank was in a catch 22; If he gave the list up he'd probably die, if he didn't, he'd still probably die. He had to buy a lil time.

"I told y'all the money was in the car, as for a list, all I got is a pick-up list and everything's accounted for."

Ramon and Fat Man didn't say a word. Ramon walked over to one of the duffel bags and unzipped it. He pulled out some KY jelly lubricate and a pair of electrical curling irons. He plugged the curlers in the socket and flipped the on switch. He then ripped the house coat off of Felicia, leaving her lying ass naked on her stomach and knees, as she whaled and shook uncontrollably.

Removing the cap off of the KY jelly tube, he applied a heavy amount in his hand and squirted some over the curling iron. Ramon then forcefully fondled Felicia's privates and stuck two fingers in her anus, violating her innocence.

"Now this is what's gone happen nigga," Ramon said, "The same way I'm finger fuckin' yo' bitch in her ass, once them curlers heat up for 10 minutes, I'm gone take 'em and do the same with your baby boy's shitter."

Pure terror filled Stank's mind.

"Stop, stop y'all win! The list is in the kitchen, in the Captain Crunch cereal box," Stank said, scared to death for his son.

Ronnie and Connie now feared for their lives if shit got too far out of hand.

"Are you sure? Because if it's not in that cereal box as you stated, then they gone have to make a new asshole for your son," Fat Man said, in a relaxed manner to let everyone in ear shot understand he had no problem making good on his threat.

"That's where it is," Stank said, "Just get it and go! Just get it and get this over with, damn," Stank said sounding like a dead man walking, with no more fight left in him.

Ramon went to the kitchen, grabbed the cereal box, and dumped the contents out. He felt like a little kid looking for the prize on a Saturday morning, before the cartoons came on. A piece of notebook paper wrapped in plastic lay on the pile of crushed cereal, along with a few scattering roaches. Ramon picked up the package, ripped the plastic off and unfolded the paper. There it was the names of all of the people of interest, along with the codes for the amount of money owed to his father.

"Got it! Ramon said from the kitchen, headed back towards the living room. "Alright this is how it's gone go down," he said looking directly at Stank, "You gone call your people and tell them what just happened."

Puzzled, Stank looked up at Ramon.

"This is an out for you, because you're stuck in the middle of something that really doesn't involve you," Ramon added.

"What happens after that?" Stank asked interested to see how it'd all play out.

"Nothin', all you have to do is leave and forget about everything," Ramon said in a nonchalant type of way.

"Sounds too good to be true," Stank said.

"My word is my bond, leave and I won't do nothin' to you," Ramon repeated with a straight face.

Stank looked to Fat Man for reassurance.

"You heard the man. Play ball and everything is everything, if not well...," Fat Man said, looking down at the baby.

"Hand me the phone," Fat Man said.

Ramon walked over to the window and Fat Man walked with Stank to make the call. He could hear Stank spilling his guts to whoever was on the other end of the line.

As soon as he hung up the phone Ramon questioned him. "What did they say?"

"They're on their way around here," Stank said.

"So predictable!" Ramon snapped as he peeped out of the blinds into the parking lot, to see the white moving van just pulling up.

"Put the baby in the crib, go to his car and get the money. Take the other bag with you. Stank, you sit your ass right there in that chair, and it'll all be over with soon," Ramon said.

Fat Man cleaned up quickly, grabbed the bag and was out the door headed towards Stank's Chevy Caprice.

In the trunk, lay a brown paper bag filled with money. He dropped the duffle bag between the white van and his Lincoln. He placed the bag of money in the back seat and headed back to the apartment. As soon as he came in, he nodded to Ramon, confirming the job was done.

"Let them up. Felicia, I'm sorry it had to go down like this. I hope you can forgive me and understand this was business not personal.

Felicia didn't say a word nor did she reach for something that would hide her nakedness.

As soon as Fat Man removed her restraints, she ran full speed to the baby's room, crying.

Ronnie and Connie followed her to make sure she wouldn't do anything stupid.

Ramon began playing with the blinds by opening and closing them a few times.

"That's the signal Ray," BooBoo said, looking over at the driver.

"Grab the shit then," Ray replied.

BooBoo opened the side door of the van and grabbed the duffel bag. As soon as he shut the door, the van pulled away from the parking lot.

"You good?" Fat Man questioned Ramon.

"Yeah man, just a lil' nervous, I guess," Ramon replied.

As he watched the van pull off, he stopped playing with the blinds.

When word spread that Ramon had been killed, Mouse went to the count-house across town on 23rd and Fairmount Avenue to clean up.

All the after-hour spots were closed immediately. Everybody with heroin packages had until noon the next day to straighten their tab, by either paying in cash or the left over drugs. The whores were the only ones to remain working, instead of giving their daily take to Gina as usual, they'd now report to Liz, who was Mouse's bottom bitch.

Teddy Bear had the number game, which Mouse couldn't touch. That was the only part of the racket he didn't work.

Mouse had the safe deposit key for the First National Bank, in which Ramon kept the books and the list. The bank managers knew if anything ever happened to Ramon, Mouse would come to the bank and clean up before the police could find the key and put it all together.

Not only was the list worth money, but for the one to possess it, it also meant power; a power Mouse had longed to have for what seemed like forever, a power he wanted to pass on to his nephew Stank.

Chapter 4

Unlike Ramon, he wanted to keep the criminal element in his bloodline forever.

"By who?" ManMan asked.

"Don't know, but we gonna find out," Mouse said.

"Tell the boys to follow me. Once we get there, make sure everything is locked and loaded. When I give the word........kill everything breathing in the whole complex!" Mouse added, as they ran to each of their cars, yelling out instructions.

"Say no more," ManMan shouted!

Mouse started up the engine to the Fleetwood, and the four-car entourage left the upper scale of West End neighborhood known as Carytown, headed for Jefferson Village.

When they entered the apartment complex, they found the street blocked off by a four-car pileup, with two men fighting and wrestling on the ground. It looked more like a huggin' match between two elementary kids more so than two grown men.

"Get this shit out the way," Mouse said to the two men in the street.

They continued to hug and toss each other around, and by now, there were a few other cars behind the armed entourage.

Fed up with the foolishness, he signaled for ManMan to get out of the car and stop the all the bullshit.

I ain't got time for this shit right here, ManMan thought, as he quickly hopped out of the car and approached the two guys in the middle of the street.

The cars behind Blue's Lincoln began blowing their horns, indicating they needed to get by or turn off.

ManMan turned and signaled for Blue to let them pass.

"Alright, calm the fuck down!" Blue yelled as if the other drivers behind him could actually hear him.

Once ManMan saw the car moving to the side, he approached the two men. "Alright shawty, y'all let this shit go," he said, as he tried to grab both men with both of his arms extended.

As soon as ManMan touched the shoulder of the first man, both men reached inside their coats, pulling out automatic pistols and both started blazing.

Boom! Boom!

Two bullets struck ManMan in the stomach and chest, followed by two more striking him in each shoulder. ManMan backed up, reaching for his own pistol.

Boom! Boom! Boom! Boom! The next four shots struck him directly in the face, cutting and tearing the flesh from his nose, right cheek, left eye, and lower chin; he was dead before he even hit the ground.

As the rest of the gunmen tried to exit their cars, they were hit by a hail of gun fire by the cars they'd just tried to let pass. The gunfire exploded from the rear left side of the cars. For that one moment in time, it sounded like Vietnam around the entire complex. All Mouse could do was try and duck down in the car's seat for cover. It was on no use, though. The slugs cut through the metal doors like a hot knife through butter, if not easier.

Rat-tat-tat-tat-tat! was all that could be heard for what seemed like twenty minutes, when in fact, it was only for less than one.

The cars sped away from the scene, leaving behind four car loads of bloody, bullet-riddled carnage and a faceless corpse in the middle of the street that was put into focus after the clouds of gun smoke cleared, with the smell of burnt rubber.

As the fog of smoke begin dissipating, Fat Man's Lincoln slowly crept out of the parking lot. Every passenger viewed the fresh homicide scene.

"Damn! What the fuck happened 'round here?" Ramon verbalized in a sarcastic manner.

"Somebody fucked up!" Fat Man added.

The three female passengers closed their eyes and turned their heads.

"Drive, drive! Get the fuck out of here!" Connie yelled out with tears in her eyes.

Fat Man thought to himself, this bitch just tried to pull rank? Now she's shook as hell? I'm gone blast this bitch when I catch her by herself.

As soon as they turned onto Midlothian Turnpike, they could hear the sirens from cop cars, ambulances, and the familiar sound of someone banging on the trunk.

"Nigga, shut the fuck up wit' all that bangin' if you ain't tryna die. I can stand no cryin' ass nigga. You better not grow up to be no tender-dick-punk like that nigga back there," Felicia said to her baby.

"My nephew a real nigga like me," Ramon said, "Just don't tell Thomas about this." The whole car burst out into laughter.

Chapter 5

"What the fuck happened here?" Detective Jason Howard asked his partner, Michael Hutch.

"I don't know, and I bet you none of them know, either," he answered, pointing at all the people aligned along the sidewalk, resembling participants in a food stamp line.

"Let us through," Detective Howard said leaning his head out of the window. They parked near a corner and got out of the car. As they neared the yellow tape where the crowds were surrounding the uniformed police, they could see people crying and whispering in the crowd. Both detectives removed their note pads along with ink pens from inside their jacket pockets. A uniform cop approached them, "This way."

"Who's in charge?" Det. Howard asked the uniformed officer.

"Sgt. Johnson, Sir," the officer replied.

"Which one?" Det. Hutch inquired.

The uniformed officer pointed out the middle aged, white man, with the thick salt and pepper mustache and pot belly.

"Thank you," Det. Hutch said as they walked towards the Sergeant.

"Don't let anyone touch anything until Forensics gets here," Sgt. Johnson said, as both detectives walked up on him from behind.

"Sgt. Johnson," Det. Howard called.

"Now what?" Sgt. Johnson's voice was echoing, and you could clearly hear his frustration.

"This is Det. Hutch and I'm Det. Howard. What do we have thus far?"

"Sorry about that Det.," Sgt. Johnson said, removing a white handkerchief from his back pocket to wipe the sweat from his brow, as he continued.

"It's just so much going on right now."

"That's alright Sargent, just get us up to speed and take a moment if you must," Det. Howard said to him.

"I can't do that. Time is of the essence fellas. So, from what we've been able to gather, it looks as if we have a massacre on our hands," Sgt. Johnson said, folding the sweat soaked handkerchief and placing it back in his pockets.

"How many victims are there in all?" Det. Hutch asked, preparing to write down the information on his pad.

"Thirteen total!" Sgt. Johnson replied in an I-don't-believe-this kind of tone.

"Thirteen!" Both detectives exclaimed at the same time, with obvious looks of astonishments on their faces.

"I haven't seen anything even close to this in my ten years of being in law enforcement. Hell, not even in my fuckin' career or life! If these guys weren't black I would've sworn this was a mob hit!"

Sgt. Johnson paused then began speaking, "How do you know it *wasn't* a mob hit?" What, you think the mob won't waste bullets on ghetto hustlers or something?" Det. Hutch asked with more than a hint of disdain in his voice. "I didn't mean to..."

"You didn't mean to what...?" Det. Hutch finished, cutting him off mid-sentence, "Put your foot in your mouth?"

Det. Hutch hated racist people, especially racist cops. He'd grown up in Churchill and remembered how the white officers used to rape the neighborhood instead of protecting it. That's why he'd pursued this career with a vision to truly do police work for the communities of the citizens who paid his salary.

"Alright boys, that's enough!" Det. Howard intervened, "We have work to do. Remember, we're the professionals here. But for future references, Sgt. Johnson, keep your personal feelings to yourself, and if you ever come out to another homicide scene, remember this, nothing and no one can be ruled out until the case is closed. Understood?"

"But I was just..." Sgt. Johnson was cut off again.

"Under-stood?" Det. Howard asked again.

"Understood and I apologize, Sir," Sgt. Johnson said, turning beet red from both embarrassment and anger. He hated being out ranked by anyone, much less two niggers. He wasn't a full-fledged redneck, but he felt like everything had its place. Times were changing and getting away from the good ole boy system. *Damn that ole Kennedy and J. Sergeant Reynolds,* he thought to himself.

"So, let's piece this together. Hutch go check for witnesses, while Sgt. Johnson here gives me the rundown as to what the evidence reflects, and no matter what, no statements to the press," Det. Howard stated, as he saw TV News vans and reporters everywhere. They stood outside of the yellow tape with their cameras, while running to get a good spot to see the crime scene.

"Chief, Chief!" they heard one reporter calling out, as the many vulture-like news people rushed Richmond's Chief of Police Harry Duling. "Oh shit, here we go," The chief mumbled aloud.

They all thought since Harry Duling was a fiend for the media's attention and hired as Chief of Police, anything good, bad, or ugly concerning the city, he had to be in front of the camera. His officers did all the work and he'd receive all the glory.

"No comment!" Chief Duling said as he entered the realm of yellow tape. "What in the name of Jesus happened here?" he asked the three of them.

"Well sir...we have thirteen homicides on our hands. The apparent cause of death seems to be gun fire." Sgt. Johnson was cut off again.

"No shit dumb dick. Everyone knows that from the bullet holes and shell casings." Chief Duling said pulling rank.

"I want answers, arrests, and convictions. Find witnesses and assure them we'll use all of our resources to protect them and make worth their while. The Mayor is watching this closely gentlemen. I expect a full report on my desk by tomorrow morning and y'all will report directly to me and no one else. I'll have to keep the Mayor informed as well as my public!"

"What the fuck does this cracker mean his public?" Det. Hutch thought.

"Understood?"

Both detectives and Sgt. Johnson all looked at one another and replied in unison, "Yes, sir!"

"Well, if you'll excuse me...my public awaits." Chief said saluting the officers. They returned salutes.

"As you were." Chief Duling said turning his back heading towards the sea of madness called the media.

"Let's get to work." Det. Howard said with Det. Hutch diving into the crowd to interview people in hopes of picking out a lotto winner or two. Howard and Johnson walked over to the first body that lay in the middle of the street under a sheet.

"So what we got?" Howard asked.

"Victim appears to be a black make about 5'10" tall and in his early to mid-twenties. No ID so we'll have to wait on a fingerprint analysis. If the victim doesn't have a criminal record, then we'll have to hope that DMV can help us locate the owner of these cars because I doubt if any of these cars are registered under any of these guys."

Sgt. Johnson said.

"What type of weapon was used?" goes Howard.

"We found shell casings belonging to a .45 automatic," Johnson replied.

Howard stood with his hands on his waist eyeing the entire horrific scene. "Okay, check for prints and run those plates." "Let's go to the cars." He says as he began walking to the car and signaling Johnson to follow suit.

When they reached the car, Mouse was hanging halfway out the front driver's side door. Det. Howard turned his head and tossed his lunch...right out his mouth.

"Don't feel bad. I done the same thing earlier," Johnson said.

The top of Mouse's head was split in half with his brain fully exposed. His left eye was hanging on the veins that attached to his brain was out of its socket. The smell of blood, death, and bowel flooded their nostrils immediately as the sheet was removed. Det. Howard gathered himself, removed a napkin from his left front pants pocket and wiped his mouth.

"Excuse me!" Howard managed to say as he took a deep breath. Johnson just nodded, "Okay what's the story?" Howard said keeping his nose covered.

"Black male 5'6" to 5'7" in height, appears to be in his late 40's early 50's with a .224 caliber casings are on the ground my guess is an AK47 or 47's." Johnson preached.

"Maybe this was a mob hit." Howard pondered in his mind.

"Any ID?" Howard asked.

"Nah, but our units are certain this is Clinton "Mouse" Jones but we'll have to wait for a positive ID." Johnson said.

"What the fuck was Mouse doing in Jefferson Village, much less dead? Mouse was a number runner, pimp, and gambler. This isn't his M.O." Howard thought.

He never had the pleasure of meeting this legend that stood by the iconic figure Ramon Baker, but he was sure this was behind something major and retaliation was surely to follow. Just what we needed; another violent crime wave to add on to the high body count.

"Let's move on." Johnson said as they continued to view the bodies of each victim, all victims of overkill. Their bullet riddled bodies were torn to pieces, missing limbs, and you can see through their backs and chests. These weren't just mere around the way or run of the mill gunmen. These were professionals. But who, besides the mob, had the resources and the money to hire such a highly trained team of pure breed killers like these.

"No witnesses," Hutch said as he approached Johnson and Howard, "but it does look like a family member of one of the victims is over there." Hutch pointed to the young girl being consoled by a few women.

"Who is she crying over?" Howard asked.

"She claims one of the victims is her father; one Clinton "Mouse" Jones. Hutch said.

"When she calms down, we will definitely have to talk with her. Johnson, make sure you get the lab results to us ASAP! Come on Hutch. We got to make a run." Howard said.

"What about Duling?" Johnson said.

"You can handle up here. Meet us at the station with your notes and we'll file the paperwork tonight. I think I may have a lead on this just trust me!" Howard said.

"Okay it's your Detective." Johnson said turning his attention back towards the crime scene.

Howard and Hutch headed for their car.

"What's up?" Hutch asked.

"I'll tell you in the car." Howard replied as they headed towards the media circus.

"Detectives, do you have any leads?" shot one reporter.

"How many victims?" shot another.

"Can you confirm that one of the victims is one Clinton "Mouse" Jones?" shot another.

"We have no comments at this time. Chief Duling will hold a press conference as soon as we make him aware of our findings and he will give the public a full briefing on all of the developments as they unfold. Thank you!" Howard said as he pushed his way to the driver side of the car, with Hutch in tow. He slammed the door, started the engine as the crowd of reporters ran back to the crime scene.

"Where to partner?" Hutch asked.

"Fairfield." Howard instructed.

"What's in Fairfield?" Hutch asked being that the crime happened over in Southside. Howard simply replied, " Answers!"

Chapter 6

Once Ramon felt how wet and warm her pussy was, he forgot all about her mouth. Not only did Connie have the bomb ass head, she possessed that snapper pussy. The type of pussy that stayed tight no matter how much she fucked and how many different sizes she fucked. That sweet pussy gripped a dick like a fist covered in crazy glue.

Connie straddled Ramon and began riding him like she was in first place of the rodeo show. She loved fucking Ramon. He had what girls referred to as that *just right* dick. Not too big. Not too small. Not too fat but just right to please all. As he entered her sugar walls, he felt the walls closing in and sucking him in deep.

"Uh oh, oh shit that's it Ramon she moaned as she started to adjust to his dick and began gyrating her hips to his movement. Ramon thrust his middle upwards to meet her hips.

"Oh yeah! Fuck me Ramon! Fuck me!" She screamed.

Her nasty talk always seemed to light fire in Ramon to give her what she wanted.

"Uh...uh...uh..ooh...I'm bout to cum! Oh shit don't stop Ramon. I'm almost there! Oh, Oh!" Her moans only made Ramon pick up the pace. He sucked on her breast and guided her hips with his hands as she rubbed her clit against his lower stomach for stimulation.

"Oh, oh, oh, fuck me! Oh fuck me Ramon!" She moaned like a whore as her left inner thigh began to tremble signaling that her orgasm was fast approaching. Ramon commenced to sucking on her breast fiercely and quickened his strokes as he felt his nutt approaching at fast speed matching his heaving breathing.

Sweat was covering Connie's forehead and hair. "Oh fuck me muthafucka! Don't stop Ramon! I'm getting ready to cum! I'm getting ready to cum. Oh shit!" She exclaimed as she was frantically bounced up and down riding his dick.

Ramon just kept stroking and thrusting his manhood up inside her wet walls, elevating his ass higher off the bed each time.

"Oh shit I'm cummin', oh shit! She moaned shooting her first blast of love juice down on Ramon's hairy dick. The first spasm of her pussy brought Ramon close to climax the second one took him over the edge. That first jolt of semen shot directly to the back of her vagina causing her to cum again. The second jolt cause Ramon to lock up from the intense Muscle spasm and the way Connie's pussy was gripping him while sucking all the life out of him for that moment. He buried his head into her breast as she shook in his arms as the waves of satisfied pleasure took them to great heights of ecstasy. Connie fell from Ramon's arms onto the side of the bed lying straight on her back.

"That was amazing," she managed to say between breaths and reeking of fresh sex.

"Fo sho!" Ramon replied wanting to say as little as possible, he like most men, wanted to savor the moment. Then find a way to get rid of her unless she wanted to suck him off.

"I have to piss" Ramon said. Getting up he turned the TV on in the room.

"Our top story tonight is the mass murder that happened over South Richmond earlier today. We have live coverage from the scene. Let's go now to our news co-respondent Charlie Young as he joins us live from the scene." Carol Smith said

"Charlie, what are the latest developments."

"Well Carol," Charlie said, "I'm live here in Jefferson Village Apartments where earlier today what many refer to as a massacre occurred. We were able to get an interview with one resident.

"I heard the gunshots but I ain't seen nothing." A black girl no more than 19 years old with a scarf over her head, a babe in one arm, a toddler holding on to one hand and one in the oven, missing one of her front teeth.

"I had my children in the hallway and we just duck down. Next thing I know these men folk was dead. I feel so sorry for the family child. She said

"What do you think should happen to the people responsible for this crime?" Charlie said,

"Well the Lord giveth and the Lord taketh away. God is the best to judge and I just pray for the souls of these men and the people who were responsible." With that said Bonita Jenkins hauled ass back to her building that was bombarded by the hail of bullets.

"As you can plainly see Carol, there seems to be no witnesses willing to come forward with information. The police have no leads and haven't disclosed any details or the names of the victims until the families have been notified." Charlie added.

"Are there any suspects?" Carol asked.

"No suspects were named." Charlie stated. "As details develop we'll keep you informed, reporting live from Channel 6 News. I'm Charlie Young. Back to you Carol." Charlie ended.

"Thanks Charlie," Carol said. "In other news..." she began reporting on different news, Ramon cut the TV off.

"Let's shower and get the fuck outta here!" Ramon said to Connie.

"Where out of town are we going Ramon?" Connie said as the mere thought of her and Ramon being on the run made her pussy wet. *Mainly because she'll be the only piece of pussy he'll have while they're on the run.*

"Nah, we just got to get outta here for right now." Ramon said trying to figure out why she wanted to leave town.

"Okay boo, but I got to take care of something before we go." Connie said getting off the bed and approaching Ramon.

"We ain't got time for no bullshit, so make it quick!" Ramon's voice was authoritative and to the point!

"Well, that'll depend on you." Connie said dropping to her knees. "You know they say the second nutt always takes a 'lil longer." Connie said smiling grabbing Ramon's dick with one hand and placing his head in her mouth while sucking on it like a blow pop as she deep throated him totally after getting him to full erection. She began making that slurping and smacking noise with her wet mouth as her head commenced to bobbing back and forth greedily tightening her jaws and sucking hard. Ramon nearly collapsed when he shot his load off in the back of her throat. She sucked harder making his knees tremble and shake. Connie swallowed every drop of this offspring as he fell back up against the wall clearly done!

"Didn't you say we can't waste no time? So put some pep in your step." Connie said getting up off her knees knowing she had clearly pleased her man. She was already in the shower by the time Ramon had gathered himself.

"I love this bitch for all the wrong reasons" he said to himself as he entered the bathroom to join her in the shower.

"'Bout time!" Connie said as she heard him step in the bathroom.

"Just keep your hands to yourself so we can get up outta here." Ramon said knowing he couldn't afford to think with his dick. Not right now.

"Okay, but tomorrow night...you're all mine, right?" She asked.

"My word is my bond." Ramon answered. After dropping Connie off, Ramon headed straight to Downtown Southside.

He had to make sure everything was in order. He got to his destination in about fifteen minutes at 1926 Lenmore Street; the perfect spot for their business. Ramon parked Fat Man's Lincoln on the side of Ingram Street. As soon as he turned the corner, he sees the white van Ray and Boo Boo drove earlier. Rage overtook him.

"What the fuck are these niggas thinking?" Ramon thought as he got out of the car he made a bee line straight to the house that sat on the corner. Looking around to make sure no cops was 'round, he knocked on the door in code to let them know it was a member of the team. Boo Boo unchained and unlocked the door. The door was half way open when Ramon punched Boo Boo square in the jaw, "crack!" dropping him like a bad habit.

"What the fuck is this shit doing 'round the corner?" Ramon barked out.

"What shit?" Boo Boo asked while nursing his jaw.

Ramon pulled his gun from his waist. I swear Ramon I don't know what you talking about shawty. It ain't gotta be like that! For real!" Boo Boo pleaded with Ramon.

Fat Man entered the living room stopping Ramon from pulling the trigger.

"Hell naw, shawty! What you doing?" Fat Man asked with a slight raise in his voice.

"These dumb muthafuckas left the van parked 'round the corner." Ramon said.

"Bullshit, Hank took the truck to Brookfield and set it on fire. "Boo Boo said while taking his left hand trying to re-adjust his jaw bone. "Did you see him set it on fire?" Ramon asked both Boo Boo and Fat Man. "nah, but he said he," Boo Boo was cut off mid-way through the sentence.

"He ain't do shit! Where Ray at?" Ramon asked.

"In the back with Liz!" Fat Man said. Ray came from the back pulling his pants up.

"What's up bruh?" Ray said. The look Ramon had in his eyes was pure fury. If Ray hadn't come from the same lanes as Ramon, he would surely be dead by now.

"Why did you send Hank to take care of that, when it was your job?" Ramon asked.

"He needed to get his feet wet and the job was major but not hard." Ray said.

"A major league job and you send a rookie. I can't believe this shit." Ramon said in disgust.

"You know that's lil bruh you talking about." Ray said out of honor of his blood and my backing his candidate.

"Well lil bruh, left the job undone so it falls back on you. Mistakes come with a price, so Boo Boo will get half of your gap." Ramon said with no emotion and all business.

"Boo Boo go take care of that, and my bad for hittin you Cuz. Ramon continued,

"Mistakes bring down empires. Daddy made a mistake and it cost him his life." Ramon said pointin' to the back room.

"They come a dime a dozen and in some places cheaper than that." Ray and Fat Man were speechless. Boo Boo fully understood before leaving he turned to Ramon.

"Dog, I'll remain loyal to the cause but trust is all I ask. The punch was nothing, but until I'm a Ramonral in this army, I follow orders. I'll never break the chain of command." As he shut the door behind him and went to dispose of evidence.

"Okay where the nigga at?" Ramon said.

"This way." Fat Man answered pointing to the hallway that leads to the kitchen. Leading the way, Fat Man opened the door on the left that lead to the basement. Fat Man hit the light switch on the wall as all three men walked down the old wooden steps. It was dark and smelled like straight mold from the water damage caused by out-dated plumbing.

"Mm mm mm!" Stank was trying to speak through the gag in his mouth. He jumped around in the wooden chair he was tied to, it was no use; he couldn't escape.

"Big Bank Stank, your ass still running your mouth knowing damn well can't nobody hear your ass!" Ramon said laughing at the helpless prey. Ramon removed the blind fold and saw pure terror in his eyes.

"Tell us what we want to know and you good, if not well..." Ramon said looking at Ray to drive his point home.

"Understand?" Ramon said. Stank just nodded his head before Fat Man removed the old wash cloth from his mouth. Stank struggled to get the foul stale taste out of his mouth.

"Water, please water." Was all he managed to say as Stank tried to clear his throat. Ramon gave Ray the okay to get the water. Ray hurried up the steps as Ramon began to interrogate Stank further.

"I gave you my word that I wouldn't harm you, all I want is Mouse's stash house and his safe house." Stank never thought he'd be in this situation when he woke up this morning. Ray was on his way back down the steps when Stank decided he better talk.

"Okay he has 5 spots total. The list is where the answers are, but you got to know how to decipher codes. If I could see the list I could tell you where everything is. But it's a trick to everything. The money will only be trusted to me and the people holding the money have their own hiding places. So you'll...." *SMACK!* Stank felt the whole right side of his face sting and then grow numb as a trail of blood leaked from his bloody mouth.

"Nigga we ain't playing no mo games here. What the fuck you think this is." Ramon said massaging the back of his right hand.

"Now one last time, where the fuck them houses at and which is which." Ramon barked. Stank knew it was no use trying to play dumb so he began to come clean." It's only 4 spots all of them are across the street from each other." Stank said holding his head down. He was beaten, tied, starving and sick of the whole shit.

"What's the set up?" Fat Man asked.

"The houses are on Tallwood in the middle of the block. There are look outs on both street corners and the end of booth alleyways. During the day two old women sit on the porch of each corner house. All the money is moved and handled by elder women." Stank said. Ramon drew his hand back to hit him again.

"For real! I'm not bullshitting, man." Stank said bracing himself for another blow.

"Hold up!" Fat Man said.

"Let him finish" Ramon shot Fat Man a look like

"You believe this shit"

"I know it sounds crazy. But he got the idea from your daddy. It's logic behind it. The old women have children and grandchildren in the streets, but everybody is on payroll. So if somebody tries to rob the old women they'll never make it off the block because it's business and personal. Think what one of us would do if a street punk robbed one of our parents or grandparents." Stank explained. It made sense to Ramon because his father learned from Jelly Bean.

"As long as everybody eats, nobody is hungry. Most of all not even a vicious dog will bite the hand that feeds him."

"Inside?" Fat Man asked "Inside what?" Stank asked dumbfounded.

"Inside the houses jackass!" Ramon responded.

"Oh, each house has round the clock gunmen. Those old guys that you think are washed up pimps are hired guns," Stank answered.

"So how is the money moved?" Ramon asked.

"The old women carry it on them in their girdles, under those oversized church dresses." Stank said while sucking the blood back into his mouth.

"Drop offs and pickups, every morning at 10 o'clock. At the corner store called the mar-ket." Stank paused again to suck his own blood.

"The bread truck drops off the dope and picks the money up, then goes back to J.N.W.'s Bakery. That's the headquarters. As to who the connect is, I don't know. But it has to be someone up high because Uncle Mouse never spoke on 'em. That's it, that's all I know." Stank felt relieved to have gotten the information out and now it was time to be rewarded for his favor.

"So now that I co-operated can I go?" Stank begged.

"First we'll have to check it out and if it's on the up and up, you'll get what you've earned. My word is my bond." Ramon said.

"I'm hungry and I have to use the bathroom." Stank cried.

"Look at this bitch ass nigga" Ramon thought

"But a dead man is useless to me now."

"Fat, get him something to eat. Have Liz bring a bed pan for Stank." Ramon said.

"No problem but let me holla at you upstairs." Fat Man said. "Hold tight babe boy everything will be fine." Ramon said as the two men headed upstairs. Soon as the door was shut Fat Man turned to Ramon.

"Why the fuck you saying names around this chump if you ain't gone kill him?" Fat Man said to Ramon with fury in his voice.

"First of all I can say whatever I want to a dead man." Ramon said.

"But you gave your word that you won't gone kill him." Fat Man was cut off.

"I'm not gone lay one hand on em. Once we check this shit out and make sure shit is real. Then my good friend, you are going to kill him." Both men bust out in laughter.

As Detectives Howard and Hutch pulled away from the corner of Fairfield Ave. and 22nd St, the old man closed the door. Lighting his Cuban cigar he headed into the study and shut the door.

"Gentlemen we have a serious problem. I was just informed that Mouse is no longer with us." Tank Williams informed the room of elite men.

"What happened?" Irish, Jerry, and Monae asked.

"Details are sketchy. However it appears that he was ambushed by gunfire. But my resources assure us that our business venture is protected and nothing has been breached. Operations will continue as planned. Now if you gentlemen will excuse me, I have an urgent matter to attend to." Jack said as the 7 men known as the commission left his house.

Timothy "Tank" Williams was born in Greenville, South Carolina. He had earned a scholarship to play football at Norfolk State University and had earned the nickname Tank from his day of playing fullback in college. He was rated as the best full back in the nation beating out Jim Brown as a pro-football prospect. But he blew his knee out the last game of his senior year of college playing Virginia State University during homecoming weekend. His brother was a friend of Frank Lucas that was connected to Bumpy Johnson. His brother introduced him to Bumpy Johnson and he handled the entire heroin distribution from Virginia to South Carolina for them. After Bumpy's death, he and Frank Lucas carried an ongoing friendship that sent a deadly supply of heroin to the south. Ramon Baker Sr. and Clinton "Mouse" Jones were his underbosses. Now with both Ramon and Mouse dead, he'd hope that Stanley "Stank" Jones was ready to take over. He picked up his telephone and dialed the number.

"Hello." a female voice said answering the phone.

"May I speak to Stank?" Tank said

"Stank isn't here." The female responded.

"Well when he comes in tell him the torch is lit and it's his if he wants it." Tank replied and then hung up. Felicia started to wonder who that was, but more importantly how much would it be worth to Ramon. The $15,000 she got for Stank was chicken food compared to this, she just hoped Stank wasn't dead yet. She dialed Connie's number hoping Ramon was in reach.

"Hello" Connie said answering the phone. "Girl I just need to holla at you." Felicia said in her ghetto girl voice.

"Wus up girl?" Connie responded hoping to hear some good gossip.

"I got a call and I need to run it by Ramon." Felicia said seeing dollar signs dancing in her head.

"I don't know where Ramon at?" Connie said

"How the fuck you don't know where your man at?" Felicia said clearly frustrated.

"Bitch, you wish you had a man to wonder about." Connie snapped back getting defensive.

"That's why I fuck other bitches' niggas and let them wonder for me and yours might be next." Felicia was a cum freak, and money made her cum harder.

"You washed up ass hoe; Ramon wouldn't fuck you with Thomas's dick." Connie said laughing at her.

"Truth be told hoe you getting my sloppy seconds; Marilyn Monroe ain't the only bitch to keep it in the family." Felicia was lying but she couldn't let no young chick straight out of high school out talk her.

"And look at where the bitch at now." Connie said sending a hidden message in her comment.

"Matter of fact hoe he just walked through the door hold on." Connie said looking at Ramon.

"Phone."

"Who is it?" Ramon asked,

"Marilyn Monroe." Connie said trying to be funny.

"Who?" Ramon said not believing his ears.

"Hello who is this?" Ramon said thinking it was a prank call or something.

"Hey boo this Felicia, I need to talk with you about a phone call I got a few minutes ago. I need you to come by here." Felicia said in a familiar ghetto flirtatious type of way.

"Look I ain't got time 'fo no bullshit." Ramon said.

"Ah this will be worth your while I promise!" Felicia said in a low sexy voice.

"Meet me at the store in 10mins." Ramon said hanging up the phone.

"You ain't going to meet that bitch." Connie barked at Ramon.

"You crazy as hell" Ramon barked back. He wasn't use to having anyone especially a female dictate who he dealt with. He had heard 'bout Felicia's fuck game and always wondered if it was as good as they say. Yet, she had a baby by his brother so to keep from crossing an imaginary line drawn he had to come up with a way to fight temptation.

"Everybody knows she's a hoe and word is that's not Thomas's baby anyway." Connie was throwing salt.

"Well that's for another day. Today, I got to know what's so important. It's too much to lose right now. Since you can't trust the broad grab your coat you're going with me." Connie was happy as a kid in the candy store with a fist full of dollars.

"You damn right I'm going."

When they pulled up to the 7-11 they saw her standing by the phone booth drinking a soda.

"He just had to bring that bitch." Felicia thought as she eyed Connie riding shotgun. Connie's smile spoke loud and clear.

"You got to come better than that." Ramon waved for Felicia to get in the car. She walked over and reluctantly opened the back door of the car and got in.

"Wus up Felicia?" Ramon said getting straight to business.

"I'm chillin!" Felicia said Ramon turned around and gave her a look indicating he wasn't in a playful mood.

"Damn you so serious. You need to loosen up a little bit; you need moms to help you unwind?" Felicia said in a soft sexy voice, while reaching for Ramon's shoulders in hopes of giving him a massage. She was cut off.

"Bitch, I'll break your fucking hands." Connie barked. "Your breaker broke?" Felicia snapped back.

"Felicia!" Ramon yelled.

"I ain't come here for no fucking games. So wus up?" His tone assured Connie he wasn't interested in Felicia's advances, but Felicia was attracted to the aggressiveness he displaced.

"Later for you bitch." she said pointing her index finger to Connie.

"Oh I'm shaking in my boots. Bitch please." Connie said rolling her eyes. Felicia wus up!" Ramon was losing his cool. Felicia smacked her lips.

"Anyway, I got a call from someone looking for Stank and I got a message for him, where he at."

"Felicia, he's in his skin, what's the message and who's it from?" Ramon said demanding more than asking.

"I don't know who's it from but it's very important." Felicia said trying to figure a way to bring the money issue up. Ramon was used to dealing with money hungry females, so he knew what was next but he played along.

"How important?" he said exhaling a little wind in his voice. "I figure it's more important than the last favor." Felicia said rolling her neck and looking at Ramon.

"Well I'll be the judge of that." He responded sharply.

"Nah, not this time boo." Felicia was on her game. She wanted her money in hand.

"You know I don't got that type of money on me but I got you once you name a reasonable price." He said trying to angle her.

"You never played stuff with me, I'm gone play fair. Just give me 15 and you owe me one." She said like she was doing him a helluva favor.

"This better be worth it." He said all business. "I don't have but 5 on me now. I'll give you that and let Connie give you the other 10 later today.

"Oh hell naw" Connie said. "I don't fuck with that bitch like that." I don't fuck with you either Connie" Felicia shot back.

"Fuck all this bullshit, this is business and if y'all can't handle business then both of y'all can care y'all ass." The car fell silent. Connie had tears in her eyes. Felicia on the other hand had the cards in her favor.

"Look Ramon, your right. This is business, so let's act professional." Felicia said as she reached into her purse to retrieve a piece of paper.

"Give me the 5 and I'll give you the message. You can have Fat Man or someone else to bring me the other 10 and you still owe me one. Felicia reasoned money in the hand beat money out of sight. Ramon handed her the 5 grand.

"Now give me the message." He demanded. Felicia unfolded the paper after putting the knot of bills in her purse, clearing her throat she said.

"The torch is lit and it's his if he wants it."

"That's it?" Ramon thought one fucking sentence.

"Fifteen thousand for that? Ramon said.

"Hell yea, I know you ain't that green." Felicia said.

"I'll give Fat Man the money and for the record, don't ever disrespect Connie like that again." Ramon said making his position clear.

"Bay you know I was just..." She was cut off by Ramon

"Just being you. Don't get it fucked up. I like you and I love having you on the team but it's certain things you just don't do to family. We all in this together like it or not, but we will respect each other. So if you like eating off this plate, make sure you use your table manners." Even though she hated rejection, she respected realness more. She envied Connie now more than ever; she'd accept her L and live to fight another day.

"That's cool Ramon. I apologize Connie but you're way too sensitive girl!" Felicia was trying to save face. She reached into her purse and pulled off two $100 dollar bills and extended them to Connie as a gesture of good faith.

"Here girl, buy you something nice. No hard feelings right?" Felicia said as Connie reached out her hand to accept both her apology and the money.

"That shit dead girl." Connie managed to say displaying a phony smile.

"Well I must be going, what time should I expect Fat Man." Felicia asked.

"He'll call you soon, probably in an hour or two." Ramon replied.

"As always it was a pleasure doing business with you, Felicia." Ramon said trying his best to sound sincere.

"Likewise, I'll holla, don't forget you owe me one Ramon." Felicia said opening the car door.

"If I did forget, I'm sure you'll remind me." Ramon responded.

"I know that's right." Felicia said laughing as she got out the car and shut the door. Ramon put the car in reverse and pulled out the parking lot.

"I can't stand that bitch!" Connie said as they pulled into traffic.

"Everybody's good for something, even people you don't like." Ramon responded.

Chapter 7

Boo Boo and Ski Bo were packed on the corner of Tallwood and Meadow Street watching the whole operation.

"This shit moves like clockwork." Boo Boo said to Ski Bo, who was busy sniffing powder coke out of a dollar bill with the edge of a match book.

"This some good shit shawty." Ski Bo replied.

"Man, get your head in the game." Boo Boo snapped. He hated that Ski Bo got high. They'd been friends since the sand box. Now they are in a very dangerous game where mistakes could cost you everything including your life. Despite his addiction, Ski Bo had always been useful and resourceful to all types of criminal activity.

"Shawty, I'm on point,." Ski Bo said, taking another sniff from his left and right nostrils.

"Them two dudes on the corner ain't moved yet. So you know they either penned us or they posted up as protection, and it's an unmarked car on the next block watching everything go down." Ski Bo said swallowing the drain of coke numbing his throat.

"Which corner?" Boo Boo said looking shook.

"And you think I ain't on point, we've been sitting here for 30mins and they were here before us. I thought you seen 'em when we parked. You slippin' man." Ski Bo said as he dipped back into the bill for another sniff.

"Put that shit up." Boo Boo said fearing he would bring attention to the car.

"Chill shawty, if they were here before us, then they not here for us." Ski Bo said calmly as ever. Boo Boo thought to himself about it and put it together in his mind, let's see what's going on." They waited to see how everything ran. Sure enough, four old women left out their homes and went to the store. On each corner, the young men hung out as they watched the elderly women closely. The bread truck had pulled up right on time. The old ladies gone inside for no more than 10 minutes and were out. On the way back to their houses, one of them stopped by the corner and handed one of the young boys a shopping bag. As soon as all the women were off the street, the young guy with the bag approached the police car.

"Look at this shit." Boo Boo said to himself aloud.

"Beautiful thing ain't it?" Ski Bo said hitting the coke again and sucking his teeth. Detectives Howard and Hutch looked in the bag nodding their heads, and pulled off from the curb. They rode directly pass Boo Boo and Ski Bo paying no attention as to who they were.

"It's more than what meets the eye." Boo Boo said starting the engine and pulling from the curb making a bee-line straight to headquarters.

"So they got the law on payroll." Ramon said after listening to Boo Boo's scouting report.

"Man this is some real organized shit." Boo Boo said putting a beer bottle to his mouth and taking a big swig. "

"Thanks for the info, I'll holla at you later dog." Ramon said giving Boo Boo and Ski Bo a pound. Both men stood up and left the house. Ramon locked the door and headed straight for the basement. Fat Man was waiting with Stank down there still tied to the chair.

"Big Bank Stank." Ramon said with excitement in his voice.

"Everything you said checked out. But you negated to mention that the police were part of the security team."

"Nah, ain't no police there until pick up day and that's only when the connect sends them by to pick up their pay off." Stank said; mad at his self for not remembering that part.

"But everything else I told you checked out right?" Stank asked to change the topic in his favor.

"Without a doubt but the connect called for you so you must know who he is." Ramon said catching Fat Man and Stank both by surprise.

"Why would he call for me, he only deals with my Uncle Mouse? I never met the connect, I swear 'fo God I don't know who he is, that's the God known truth." Stank was barring his soul and praying at the same time that these killers had some type of religion in their lives.

"Look here Stank, I'm gone level with you." Ramon said as he walked closer to Stank and got face to face with him.

"Mouse is no longer in the picture and I'm guessing you have a person to contact in case Mouse gets pinched or met an untimely fate."

"What do you mean Uncle Mouse is no longer in the picture?" Stank believed in his mind that this was some type of kidnap and ransom play to get some quick money. Death was possible but Mouse was untouchable and any hood with some sense had to know that.

"I ain't got to spell it out for ya, so here are some options. You can play ball with us like you had been doing, or you can die in a very slow and painful death. It's your call either way I'll sleep good tonight." Ramon said.

"If I give you the number of the contact would you let me go?" Stank pleaded.

"I want the connect." Ramon said. "I don't have the hook up for the connect." Stank started to sob; he felt it was truly over and it was no one that could save him.

"The connect must be very smart to be so far in the background, or you got to be the loyalist muthafucka in the world." Ramon said reaching into his coat pocket to get a notepad and pen.

"Okay Stank, give me the number and if the contact checks out we'll put everything in motion. Then I'll let you go, so you can change your life because you're not cut out for this shit." Ramon said in a manner of pity and ridicule.

"What do you mean I ain't cut out for this shit?" Stank inquired because anyone could get caught slipping.

"Well fo' one, any true thoroughbred knows you can't trust a money hungry broad. You are a tender dick ass nigga. The bitch played you out of pocket. So what do you think the wolves' gone do to you? It was only a matter of time before someone made a move on y'all. Who better than us?" Ramon said patting himself on the back. The anger in Stank was clear. *Who does this nickel and dime ass nigga think he talking to? Probably never had a thousand dollars in his pockets before. Felicia a dead bitch anyway.* He had to know if I make it out of here she's first and he's second. See how loyal Fat Man is when I have him in the chair fucking him up.

"Nigga you got me all fucked up. That bitch got out but that can happen to any nigga today which is me. Tomorrow it could be you," Stank said, with bass in his voice. Ramon looked at Fat Man and bust out laughing, which only made Stank more outraged.

"Look at Big Bank Stank, he manning up. I admire that maybe I was wrong about you after all." Ramon said wiping the smile off his face.

"But if you don't give me the number now. You won't have another chance to catch someone slippin or get caught slippin ever again." Ramon pulled his gun out to drive.

"The number is 230 7910 ask for Leo." Stank said.

"Good choice," Ramon said writing down the number he left to call the number.

"Hello" Leo said.

"May I speak to Leo." Ramon said trying his best to sound like Stank.

"This is he, with whom am I speaking to?" Leo said sounding half sleep.

"This is Stank." Ramon said

"I've been waiting on your call." Leo responded. Sounding fully awake now.

"Yea I got the message" Ramon said.

"And I'm ready for the torch to be mine." Leo was happy to hear that.

"Good, when can we meet to discuss the details of our arrangement?" Leo asked.

"Noon tomorrow is good for me." Ramon responded.

"Are you familiar with Woodfolks over Churchill?" Leo asked.

"I know where it's at." Ramon responded.

"Then noon it is, I look forward to seeing you. Sorry to hear about your Uncle, he was a good man." Leo said sympathizing with Ramon thinking it was Stank.

"Thanks for your concern. We'll talk tomorrow. Ramon said doing his best to keep his cool, as he hung up the phone.

Leo called Tank as soon as he cleared his line.

"This better be important." Tank said answering the phone.

"The rooster is in the yard headed for the hen house." Leo said.

"Let me know when he's ready to make chickens." Jack said hanging up the phone. Leo was relieved he didn't have to fill Mouse's shoes. He had a very low key figure in the organization since he ran numbers for Jelly Bean and Ramon Baker, Sr. Now he was reduced to a black businessman and the middleman between Tank and the front man. He could rest easy for tomorrow's meeting.

Meanwhile.......

Ramon and Fat Man devised a plan to hit the spot. First they'd hijack the truck full of heroin and then they'd nab the old women when they enter the store to make the exchange. Boo Boo and Ski Bo attended this meeting because they would lead the team to the capper. This will be used as a bargaining chip to gain leverage in negotiations with the connect. Leo had a 230 so he lives in Southside; he should leave the house little after 10 o'clock. By 10:30 am it'll all be over with.

"Remember fellas, keep it clean and quick. They shouldn't cause a problem. They ain't live all this time being stupid." Ramon said. "Tomorrow is the first day of the rest of our lives."

Chapter 8

As the bread truck approached the corner of Meadow and Grace Street the car in front of him stalled out. "Come on now," the driver Mook said to himself aloud, blowing the horn of the truck. Mook had just got out of prison and this is his first day on the job.

"I can't fuck this up!" he said aloud still blowing his horn. The door to the car opened up and out stepped the finest woman his eyes have ever seen.

"Damn!" Mook thought, as she went to the front of her car and popped the hood. He could see plenty of ass. His dick got hard as old Christmas candy cane. He got out the truck to assist her after flicking her hazard lights.

"What seems to be the problem?" he asked

"This cheap ass car keeps doing this bullshit." Liz answered. Reaching back under the hood he could see her cleavage exposing her ripe firm breast.

"Let me help you with that." Mook said pushing her to the side he felt the softness as her skin, the thick scent of her perfume lingered in the air despite a slight breeze and the smell of gas and oil.

"You're such a sweetheart." Liz said in her best soft and sexy voice.

"No problem." Mook went under the hood and found the problem. "Your battery cable is loose." Mook said as he used his hand to fix the problem.

"I don't know what I would've done without you. Is there something I can do to repay you," Liz said as she pulled down the front of her dress to expose more of her breast, as Mook came from under the hood of the car.

"Damn, I mean I'm sure we can think of something." Mook said as his mouth got watery. "Maybe some other time," he heard Boo Boo say from behind. Soon as Mook turned around, all he saw was the barrel of the gun. "Come on shawty not on my first day of work," Mook said thinking how bad could his luck get.

As the truck pulled up into the alley it was 9:45 am, just enough time to secure the store.

"Trucks here kinda early today," Ralph said to his partner Ramon.

"Better to be early than late," Ramon replied. Ralph and Ramon had been in business for years. When Jane Woolworth sold them the store, it was part of the deal to still allow the drugs to run through the store and they got a cut of the pie as well. If the deal was any sweeter they'd both be diabetics.

"Get everything ready," Ralph told Ramon. As Boo Boo got out of the truck, he could see that everybody was in place, and as he started to unload the truck, he could also see the young boys standing on post.

"Well here it goes," Boo Boo said under his breath as he loaded the boxes onto the dolly. Once he got inside, he noticed the store was clear of any costumers.

"Where you want these boxes?" Boo Boo said as he carried the boxes through the door.

"Who the hell are you?" Ramon asked. "I'm Mook, I just started today." Boo Boo answered.

"Where's Joe?" Ralph asked. "Out sick or something? This is my route now, if you don't want the delivery I'll just take it back on the truck, either way I still get paid." Boo Boo replied. Just place them in the backroom and wait out here because we have some products we received yesterday that have expired that we wish to return." Ramon said eyeing him kinda nervously.

"Well lucky for me I get paid by the minute and not by the hour." Boo Boo was smiling as he carried the boxes to the backroom. He heard the older women enter the store. "Hey boys," The elderly lady named Linda Sue said as she entered the store. "Joe's early today ain't he." The other elderly woman named Patrice said, as Boo Boo exited the backroom.

"You're not Joe." Linda sure said affirming that she didn't trust Boo Boo.

"No ma'am I'm not, my name is Mook, how are y'all this morning?" Boo Boo said minding his manners.

"We'd both be better if Joe was here." Patrice said with a disgustful tone in her voice.

"Well it was nice meeting y'all; if it's alright I'd like to go outside for a smoke?" Boo Boo said looking at Ramon for approval.

"Sure, Mook take your time." As Boo Boo left the store, the elderly women turned to Ralph and Ramon.

"I don't trust that joker, where did he come from." Linda Sue asked "and where's Joe?" Patrice asked trying to get information from the two men.

"I don't know where Joe is at, but this guy doesn't have a clue as to what's really going on, so let's keep it that way." Ramon said eyeing Boo Boo through the glass door.

"Ralph, keep your eye on him while we go in the back." Ramon added as he and the two old women went to handle their business. They were only in the backroom for a few minutes when they heard the words of every drug dealer's worst nightmare. "Freeze don't nobody move FBI." As soon as Fat Man seen the agents jump out and rush the store he pulled off.

"Wait until Ramon finds out about this." He thought as he stopped at the traffic light.

Woodfolks was empty except for an older looking man, a witness and a familiar looking white woman. Ramon watched carefully from across the street as the older man conversed with the white woman. It was around 11:45 am as he figured his best approach. Exactly at 11:50 am the white woman got up to leave, as soon as she exited the door, it all became clear.

"Ain't this a bitch!" Ramon thought as he seen Jane Nixon Woolworth walking to a 79 pink caddy, Coupe DeVille. JNW

Bakery it was all starting to come together. Ramon got out of the car and crossed the street scoping out the scene. As soon as he entered the door, he saw Fat Man pulling up.

"Bout time," Ramon thought as he turned around to survey the surroundings.

"Stank I presume?" he said sipping from a glass of wine and gesturing Ramon to have a seat. Ramon remained silent as he pulled out the chair and sat at the table. "Leo, I'm a man of honor first and foremost, so I'll cut to the chase." Ramon said looking Leo dead in his eyes.

"I don't deal with Indians when I can deal with the chief." Ramon said as he grabbed the bottle of wine and began to poor him a glass.

"Well it's a chain of command you have to follow Stank. I was under the impression that Mouse had groomed you for that already, but since he hasn't, I'll explain how this works." Leo was cut off. "Look middleman, since it's hard for you to read between the lines, this ain't Stank you are dealing with." Ramon said, sippin' his wine.

"Secondly, you tell that white bitch that my daddy was good enough for her to fuck so his son has to be good enough for her to do business with." Leo thought the uncanny resemblance was familiar.

"So which one are you?" Leo said sitting back in his chair. "I'm Ramon," he responded. "Okay so you're going against your father's wishes and getting into the business?" Leo asked.

"The business. You mean our business. I done took over the business. I'm sure the bitch told you that the FBI just raided the market and that she's waiting to hear more. Leo wondered how he knew about that. "Well this is what happened, federal agents kicked in the door of the store.

"Everybody get on the floor now." Agent Barns said as he entered the backroom. Ramon was trying to reseal the boxes with tape as Linda and Patrice tried to stuff the money back in their girdles.

"Put your hands where I can see em." Agent Barns said pointing his gun back and forth between the two women and Ramon.

"Just don't shoot." Ramon said with his hands in the air. "Lord Jesus don't shoot." Linda Sue said following Ramón's lead. Patrice said a prayer under her breath as tears flowed from down her face. "Girl get your hands up," Linda Sue said to Patrice hoping that the federal agent didn't shoot.

"Old lady please get your hands up or I'll be forced to exert extreme measures." Agent Barns said as Patrice raised her hands.

"Is anyone else in the store?" he asked.

"No, it's just us." Ramon said as more agents entered the backroom.

"Are you sure?" He asked again.

"Yeah yeah I'm sure." Ramon answered as the other agents escorted Ralph to the back.

"Agent Williams," agent Barnes said.

"Yes, sir." She answered.

"Search these women for weapons." He responded.

"Lord Jesus, I ask of you Heavenly Father." Patrice began to pray aloud as agent Williams frisked her for weapons, she felt the girdle.

"Got something." She said removing knots of money with rubber bands around them.

"What do we have here?" Agent Barns said as she pulled the money out like a string of yarn, will it ever end.

"Shame on you, got these old women in here doing wrong." He said to Ramon.

"Clear here." Agent Williams said as she started towards Linda sure.

"Oh hell naw, you not gone handle me and get your jollies off and try to freak me. I'm a God fearing woman. I'll just hand this stuff over. Just don't shoot." She said as she began to dump the contents of the girdle out. It had to be close to $80,000 cash on her.

"What's in these boxes you were trying to re-tape?" Barnes asked as he ripped one of them open. Inside were packages of plastic bags filled with heroin.

"Well, well, well, looks like we done stumbled upon a major drug operation." Barns said looking at Armor and Ralph.

"In the bakery. Get that driver in here now." Barns barked, as agents rushed Boo Boo into the room.

"Is this your shit boy?" Barnes asked.

"Hell naw, I just drive and drop off boxes. What's in em I don't know? Shit I just started today." Boo Boo said.

"So you mean to tell me that you don't know what your transporting, huh?" he asked Boo Boo.

"Hell naw." Boo Boo answered.

"Take his ass downtown. He'll talk. We're finished here." With that Boo Boo was gone out the room, handcuffed and thrown into a squad car.

"Now fellas we can do this the hard way or the easy way. Y'all can give me all the dope now or we can tear this store up from top to bottom costing thousands of dollars in repairs." Barnes said looking at the two men.

"The dope is in these boxes to your right and on the table. The money is to your left." Ralph said as Ramon eyed him down with a death threat type stare.

"Smart Man, is any of this money from food stamp fraud." Barnes asked.

"Hell no." Ralph said

"This is all dope money?" Barnes asked again.

"Hell no, ain't no food stamp money! This is all dope money." Ralph said frustrated that the operation had blown up.

"Agent Williams let me speak with you." Barnes said pulling her to the side. Ramon, Ralph, Linda Sue and Practice wondered what was next. Agent Barnes returned.

"I got some good news and some bad news." Barnes said.

"I'll give you the bad news first. We have to confiscate all of the drugs and the money. However, here's the good news. Our search warrant was for food stamp fraud, so by law we can't arrest y'all."

"Thank you Jesus." Linda Sue said falling to her knees praying.

"Hallelujah!" Patrice said jumping around in a circle like she'd been hit by the Holy Ghost.

"But if you get on the phone and call anyone, we'll take you down because then you're part of a conspiracy." Barnes said as the agents loaded everything into the truck and pulled off.

"That sure went smooth." Ski Bo said looking at Liz as they drove back to south side.

"So as you see Leo, I am in the business." Ramon said with a smirk on his face.

Leo was so impressed that he could devise a way to rip them off in such an elaborate scam.

"So where does that leave us at?" Leo asked.

"It doesn't leave us anywhere. You're a middleman, so you're the first to go. Tell the bitch to set up a meeting and bring her books because everything my daddy owned, I'm about to own. Ramon was now feeling full of himself. Cocksure that this washed up player would retire while he still had an out.

"Your daddy didn't own shit. All your daddy owned was an outstanding debt he incurred from Jelly Bean. Your Uncle Jelly Bean was a good hustler. Excellent really, but that young girl Boochie, took off with 3.5 million dollars of product. So if your daddy wanted to keep his family in the house y'all call home, he had to pick up the tab and put the other houses in an escrow account so to speak. That's how the bitch you speak of became so instrumental in this operation. The house is free and clear but until the other 2 million is paid off, Jane Woolworth will retain possession of the estate."

Leo said while taking a sip of wine.

Ramon felt as if he'd been hit with a ton of bricks.

"But how could that be with all the hustles he had. Y'all should've been had that money back." Ramon said.

"Everybody has to get paid, you have to maintain a certain standard of living and still pay your tab. That's business the true American way." Leo said grinning at Ramon like a Chester the cat.

"Mouse was rippin' us off." Ramon snapped.

"Probably, but the debt was on your daddy. But that's water under the bridge. What you need to do is tell me why I should let you live long enough to sell *our* dope. Oh and in that word "our" you're not included." Leo said with a light chuckle.

Ramon joined in on the laughter.

"Boy you sure are funny. I like the way you put that "our"! That was real slick boy, you're a witty guy." Ramon loudly stated as they both kept laughing.

"Well check this out," Ramon continued as his laughs came to a halt. "The reason I will live long enough to sell my dope and I do mean my dope is because I have the list.

Leo's laughter came to a sudden stop.

A young waitress came over to take their order.

"Are you fellas ready to order?"

"Nah, you can come back later cause as you can see, my friend here has enough egg on his face." Ramon said pointing at Leo. As soon as the waitress walked away, Leo was puzzled. "How did you...better yet, how do you know about the list?"

"It doesn't matter. It's just something I ran across unexpectedly. Since this is business, tell the producers of this drama, that I got the script and that I read over it thoroughly. It seems like they have invested too much in the film to scrap the movie and allow another studio to pick it up. Also, tell them when they ready to start filming, I know some good distributors. So...as they say in the industry, "Don't call me, I'll call you." Ramon said getting up and walking out the door.

Chapter 9

Detective Howard listened closely to Linda Sue and Patrice address their concerns.

"At my old age, I can't take having a scare like this." She said while nursing a cup of coffee, Brandy, and milk.

"The Federal Government is not to be toyed with." Patrice added while sittin' her cup down.

"I assure you ladies that nothing will come of this. It's just a big misunderstanding. I have contacted my people at the FBI Headquarters in Quantico, Virginia and they assured me that the store wasn't under investigation for Food Stamp Fraud." Det. Howard said while pouring his own cup of coffee Brandy and milk.

"But I know what I seen. They had the jackets, the badges, hats, and handcuffs!" Patrice exclaimed.

"Yeah I know, but it's no paperwork to confirm any of this. So I assume that we've been had being that there are no agents out of Richmond field office by the name of Barnes or Williams." He told the two elderly women.

"So, if it wasn't the FBI, then who was it?" Linda Sue asked.

"We have an idea and we're pursuing the leads as we speak but I assure you that you both have nothing to worry about. It should be business as usual." Det. Howard as he got up to leave. "You ladies have a nice day and thank you for your time and hospitality." He stated as he was closing the door.

Det. Hutch was waiting outside in the car.

"Wus up partner? Are they still down?" Det. Hutch asked excitedly.

"I think so, but we have a different player in the game now. If he's anything like his father, we'll have enough money set aside in a year or two to walk away very rich men." Det. Howard said to his partner as he started the engine.

"Who are you talking about?" Det. Hutch questioned his partner with a look that displayed concern.

"You'll know soon enough." Det. Howard said.

"This is dispatch to H-20." The radio dispatcher said.

"This is H-20 go ahead dispatch." Det. Hutch said.

"We have a 187 in the alley of Warwick and Lynnhaven Avenues, the dispatcher responded. "Copy that. We're in route." Det. Hutch said. As the car speeded across the Robert E. Lee Bridge headed over Southside.

Ronnie and Felicia stood butt naked in the kitchen of her Jefferson Village apartment.

"Damn this shit strong!" Ronnie said as she emptied the packages of heroin on the table.

"I can't believe this nigga got me butt naked in my own shit cuttin' this damn dope." Felicia's attitude was Stank!

"Shit, in a minute you'll have enough money to buy these broke down apartments." Ronnie said bursting out in laughter through her surgical mask that they both wore to keep from gettin' high of the fumes.

"Pass that morphine over here gurl." Felicia yelled out through the mask.

"This shit is fresh off the boat, too. I wonder how many times we can step on it." Ronnie stated.

"Gurl, I don't even give a fuck! I just want this shit out of here." Goes Felicia wishing she would've stayed in school and went on to college; instead, she wanted the easy money the dope game brings to females from the hood that drug dealers are attracted to.

At first she would tease and get minor money. Then she fell for Leonard Hancock, a young hustler from Mosby Court projects. He introduced her to the finer things in life and made her the envy of most school girls her age. Her nose was so open you could have driven a flagship through it. He was her first everything. She chased behind him so hard that she dropped out of school just to keep tabs on him. But as the saying goes, too much of anything isn't good for you. They eventually broke up but she was use to the life. She tried to make him jealous at first by fucking with other drug dealers but her heart belonged to Leonard. No matter whom she was with or who he was with, they still slept with each other when time was permitted.

Days quickly turned to years by that time and she was in over her head. Dogging lames and getting dogged by those with game. Sadly, she and Leonard never got back together; he ended up moving to North Carolina with a white girl. Leaving her here to fend for herself in the life she chose and grew to love.

"We need a tester." Ronnie said as a master of the game.

Her first drug boy was a kingpin. She was the shit at one time. At 15, she drove to school in a 300E Mercedes, but got a crash course in the life real quick. Her boyfriend was Michael Barnes. He controlled the heroin for Jelly Bean for years. He taught her how to cut the dope by the time she was

16, she was a master and highly sought after for her skills. But her heart belonged to Michael.

Eventually, he started to use his own product and lost everything near and dear to him. Ronnie held on for as long as she could, but she found no sense in beating a dead horse.

"Where we gonna find one of them at?" Felicia asked.

"Don't worry about a tester." Fat Man said as he entered the kitchen.

"Y'all just put a two on it and if we need to step on it again, we will. He said covering his face to avoid getting high himself.

"Fat, you finish counting that money already." Ramon shouted from the bedroom.

"Hell naw! I'm tired so I took a break." Fat Man answered.

Well, you need to break your ass back in here and finish this shit up." Ramon said laughing from the other room.

"Damn, I'm tired of counting this shit. Y'all just remember what I said. I got to go help King Ramon finish up." Fat Man said as he walked into the living room.

"I heard that shit nigga!" Ramon said as everybody started to laugh.

"...one hundred twenty-five thousand, nine hundred fifty-eight, fifty-nine, sixty. Damn! That's all of it," Fat Man said as he counted the last stacks of money he got up and flipped the empty box upside down.

"So Ramon, what's the final count?" He said as he leaned back on the couch clearly exhausted.

"With what you just counted man, we have a grand total of six hundred seventy five thousand. After we pay everybody off, we could have two hundred grand a piece and a kilo and a half of heroin each." Ramon answered.

"Ronnie and Felicia come here!" Ramon yelled as the two women half-dressed walked into the room. He grabbed four stacks of bills off the coffee table and gave each of them two separate stacks.

"That's four thousand for each of you." Ramon said with a smile on his face. Both women instantly lit up like Christmas trees. Felicia was so excited, her crotch got moist.

"Thanks Boo!" Both women managed to say at the same time while bending over to kiss Ramon on the cheek.

"Damn, y'all act like Ramon the only one that gave y'all some money." Fat Man said as both women rushed over and gave him the same treatment.

"Look, ain't no shopping taking place right now with that money. Nothing will be spent until we move this product or at least half of it." Ramon locked gazes on everybody's eyes.

"Shit, I got bills to pay." Felicia said.

"What bills?" Ramon casted a puzzled look at her. "This is a Section-8 apartment. All you pay is rent and that ain't no more than $75 fuckin' dollars!" Ramon got up and approached Felicia to address his concern.

"It's thinking like that that leads to staying where you are at now. Here's a news flash. No matter how good your pussy is, no matter how good you look, cook, or suck a dick...ain't nobody goin take care of you if you ain't trying to take care of yourself. So you can buy all the fly shit to make you feel like you the shit. But unless this inside matches the outside, you'll always be another piece of ass!" His works stung Felicia and it was evident from the tears in her eyes.

"Now listen up again! We gonna move this product and I promise you, you'll have all the shine you want to have."

Ramon called every member of his team one by one to come get their gap. Never calling one until the other one left, stressing to them the same thing he expressed to Felicia. He then sent Liz to get Benny. Benny had shot dope for years.

He could tell by the way the dope smelled in the cooker how good it was and what type of cut was on the dope.

When they arrived at the house on Lenmore Street, Benny was eager to taste test the product.

"This better not be no bullshit. I ain't got time to waste, you know." Benny said talking that old dope fiend shit. But, neither Benny nor any other dope fiend is to be taken lightly. It's not uncommon for a dope dealer to die at the hands of a dope fiend. Too much cut could leave a man dead in the spot he stands if an addict is sick and done spend his or her last or if an addict has been spending money faithfully and needs a fix until he can make a move and the dope dealer doesn't play fair. Benny is that type of addict.

Ramon was not trying to hear the shit. "Man, just let me know what I got!" He said handing Benny a thirty dollar bag of dope. Benny said down at the table and pulled his works out of his coat pocket.

"Give me some water." Benny said without even looking up, as he examined his needle. Liz went to the kitchen and returned with a cup of water.

"Thank you!" Benny said as he continued to go to work. He ripped opened the package and poured the contents into a sliver tarnished spoon. He then added some water to the heroin in the spoon. He lit two matches and placed them under the spoon for a few seconds as the mixture came to a boil. Benny then blew the matches out and grabbed his needle, sticking it in the spoon and sucking the mixture into the needle. Being careful not to overdo it, he only used about 10cc's.

"Liz, tie me off." He said as he plucked the needle.

Liz grabbed the piece of tan rubber and wrapped it around his arm. Benny then smacked his arm to find a killa vein to mainline the shot. As soon as he found one, he stuck the needle into his arm. A little bit of blood spilled into the needle as he drew back on it. He pulled back a lil more and then pushed a'lil of the mixture into his vein. Benny quickly turned back to the first time he had shot dope. *Like most users, he was scared to shoot dope because he didn't know how it'll make him feel and like most users, he hated that he fell in love with the way it made him feel. The first time is the best high after that, you began to chase something you'll never catch along with the physical sick effects and the fact that your body builds a tolerance to the small amounts. But the heroin that's in his arms now, had taken him back to the almost catch the first high. Oh, how he relished this feeling.*

The bliss he so enjoyed...

"Smack, Smack!" he heard and felt across his face along with someone pounding on his chest.

"Benny, Benny!" Fat Man yelled as he continued to beat on his chest. Benny opened his eyes and took a deep breath. Everyone breathed a sigh of relieve.

"Damn boy, you like to have been outta here," Ramon said as he leaned over the sink to catch his breath and turned on the faucet. Benny looked around and found he was naked in a tub of ice. The last thing he remembered was shooting the dope.

"Why y'all ain't shoot me up with salt water?" Benny asked as if they should've known.

Everybody looked dumbfounded at each other

"That's what you do when people OD or y'all just got some shit and don't know what y'all got." Benny said.

"If we didn't need a reading on the dope your ass wouldn't had went out. Next time muthafucka, you need to be on point yourself 'cause if we didn't know at least one method to possibly bring your ass back, we would've had to dump your ass off." Ramon said before splashing water on his face.

"You alright Benny?" Fat Man said with a lil more concern than Ramon.

"Yeah, I'm good babe boy. Let me put some clothes on and get this cold ass ice off my nutts." Benny replied lifting himself out of the tub.

Benny started noddin' as he put his clothes on.

"How long was I out?" he asked.

"Probably like five minutes." Ramon said.

"Thanks for not letting me die..." he stopped mid-sentence and went into a nod.

"Benny, you good?" Fat Man asked.

"Stop yellin'. I heard you nigga. You are fuckin' up my high fo' real. Like I was saying', thanks for bringing me back and I suggest you put a 7 on this here or you gone kill a muthafucka fo'sho!" The average user can do a whole bag of dope. Benny hadn't shot but 3 of the 10 cc's he had in his needle. This was raw. Not 100% but as raw as you're going to find on a street level.

"Alright Benny. That's a good look babe boy." Ramon said slipping him a hundred dollar bill.

"Damn that!" Benny said. "Give me another pill or two of that raw."

Even a near death experience isn't enough to make some addicts pull it together and fly straight.

When Ramon, Ronnie, and Fat Man pulled into the parking lot of Jefferson Village apartments where Felicia stayed, they saw a brand new money green Cadillac Coupe DeVille with 30 day tags.

"That shit is fly as hell!" Ronnie said. "I got to meet that nigga there. I know he high rollin' for real." She added.

"I wonder what lot he got that off of." Fat Man said.

"And do they got any more." Ramon added as everyone in the car started laughin'.

They got out of the car with a few shoppin' bags containing the morphine base and lactose they would need to cut the heroin. As they walked into Felicia's apartment, they were greeted by an unfamiliar sight.

"What the fuck?" Ramon said as he opened the door.

"What you don't like it?" Felicia said getting up off her brand new cream leather sofa. The whole living room had a makeover including Felicia. She had on a Liz Claiborne silk dress to compliment her hour glass figure. Her hair styled and freshly relaxed. She had a fresh French manicure and pedicure with freshly painted coats of red nail polish. A big screen floor model color television along with a new stereo system and a glass coffee table with matching end tables.

"What the fuck is wrong with you?" Ramon asked slammin' the front door behind him.

"I needed a new look, so don't start shit with me Ramon." Felicia said rolling her eyes and picking up a joint of reefer she was smoking before they came in.

"You gonna need more than a new look if you don't send this shit back. What did I fuckin' tell you?" He shouted clearly heated by her disobedience.

"You not my man and you don't pay no bills! Shit, you ain't even fucking me, and even if you were doing one or all of the above, you can't tell me what the fuck to do in my mutha..."

"Bam!" Before she could get the last word out of her mouth, Ramon hit her with a short right hook taking her off her feet knocking her to the floor flat on her back. "Nigga, you done lost your fucking mind. Don't no muthafucka put their hands on me." Felicia said with teary eyes as pain sot down her jaw. She reached for the box cutter from off the coffee table as she was getting up. Before she knew it, she had two pistols pointed at her.

"Bitch, I wish you would!" Ramon said with the .38 snub nose locked in between her eyes as Fat Man had his .45 automatic to the side of her head.

"Felicia, just put the blade down before we do something we don't wanna do." Fat Man said.

"Speak for yourself." Ramon coldly stated.

"You'll kill me? Your nephew mother?" Felicia said with pain in her eyes and voice in disbelief.

"You were getting ready to kill your son's uncle." Ramon replied cocking the hammer on his pistol.

"Com'on dog. You sho' you wanna do this?" Fat Man said then continued on. "Felicia drop the fuckin' blade." Fat Man yelled at them both.

"Gurl, think about your son. For the love of God gurl, think about your son." Ronnie pleaded with tears streaming down her face.

Felicia then thought twice about her actions and finally dropped the box cutter then walked over to her sofa rubbing her jaw.

"You ain't as dumb as you look." Ramon said lowering his gun.

Fat Man lowered his gun and gave a sigh of relief.

"Felicia, I'm not your man and I'm sorry for hittin' you. It's just we are in the major leagues. No time for rookie moves." Ramon said as he sat down beside her on the sofa.

"Y'all excuse us for a minute." Ramon said looking at both Fat Man and Ronnie.

"Yeah, sure; matter of fact, we gone run to the store. Y'all want anything?" Fat Man offered as he and Ronnie headed for the door.

"Nah, I'm good. How bout' you?" Ramon asked Felicia.

She just shook her head as she sat with her arms folded across her breast with tears running down her face.

"We'll be back in a minute." Fat Man said shutting the door behind them.

"Look," Ramon began. "It ain't that I don't got no love for you. It's just that besides my blood and Fat Man, you're like my blood."

"What about Connie?" She asked Ramon looking him directly into his eyes.

"What she got to do with this?" He asked.

"She's got everything to do with this. You don't have her doing half the shit for you that you got me doing." Felicia said pouting her lips.

"She's not really in this fo 'real. I mean she don't know everything like you do." He said as he wiped the tears off her cheeks. His mere touch made her feel the comfort she always longed for from Ramon.

"So what you're saying is that she don't know everything, huh?" she asked.

"Nah, I can't and don't tell her everything." Ramon began feeling the temperature rising in the room to greater heights.

"So what went down tonight won't leave this apartment?" She asked as she turned her body to totally face him.

"I'm not gonna tell her. I feel bad about all of this anyway." Ramon said noticing Felicia moving in closer to him.

"Ramon, I didn't meant to upset you, but all I wanted was some undivided attention from you." She then seductively began licking her lips.

"It's other ways to get my attention than trying to bump heads with me." He then began backing away.

"I can't tell, like what?" Felicia asked as she moved in for the kill penning him back to the sofa.

Ramon pushed her away.

"You know we can't do this." He said getting up.

"Why not?" She asked getting up and approaching him again.

"Who's going to know?"

"I will and you will. That's enough." He said.

"I don't kiss and tell." She grabbed Ramon around the neck trying to kiss him. Ramon was about to give it to her when the phone rang.

"I got it!" He said while breaking Felicia's embrace to avoid her further advances. "Hello," he said picking up the receiver.

"We're ready to start filming when you are." The voice on the other end of the phone said as Ramon held up one finger telling Felicia to hold up one minute. This was her chance. She shook her head. She wasn't going to let her prey get away that easy.

"Well, give me a location and I'll come with the treatment." Ramon said trying to push Felicia off as she dropped to her knees and unbuckled his pants.

"Tomorrow at Glenn's Diner; are you familiar?" The faceless voice said, as Ramon stopped fighting off this temptation he could no longer resist.

"Yeah, I know where it's at. What time? Ramon asked as Felicia put him inside her mouth and swallowed him slow and deep.

"Is 10:00am good for you?" goes the voice as Ramon was in ecstasy from receiving this good head from Felicia.

"Yeah, yeah. That's good. He answered talking more to Felicia than he was to the person on the phone.

"See you then." The faceless person said then hung up the phone.

As soon as Ramon heard the busy signal, he moaned, "Oh, that's it right there," as he ejaculated into her waiting mouth. Ramon quickly recovered as Felecia got up, finally getting a piece of the man she desired.

"You know this doesn't change anything." Ramon said to her as he zipped up his pants and adjusted his clothes.

"Once you get the total package, it will." Felicia said smiling at him.

"Nah, I didn't mean between us. I'm talking about all this new stuff." He then began reminding her by pointing his arm in a circular motion around the apartment.

"Damn, Boo! I really want this stuff." She said pouting her lips.

"After we move this work, I promise you can get it all back. Even better this than this...just not now." He replied trying to compromise because she was one up.

"Ok, but you gotta buy it for me." She had to find common ground.

"I got you." He said.

"A'ight, but I'm keepin' the car," she said as he headed for the bathroom.

"That's the least you can do for hittin' me in my mouth so damn hard." She said.

"I told you I was sorry for that," he said.

She turned around smiling and said,

"Nah, I ain't talking 'bout the first time. I'm talking 'bout the second time." Pointing at his crotch turning and walking into the bathroom.

As soon as she closed the door, Fat Man and Ronnie returned from the store.

"Everything cool in here?" Fat Man asked.

"Yeah, everything's good. She's getting herself together." Ramon answered.

"Good, cause we are all on the same team. But on the real Ramon, you got to stop being so demanding. What good is money if you can't spend it?" Ronnie asked with a slight chuckle.

"If you spend money and ain't got none coming it you gone eventually be broke. Furthermore, we could get tore off before we sell any of this shit then what? We ain't got no money to fight the case that's what." Ramon continued, "Nobody thinks about getting caught for a crime before, during, or after the crime. So more times than not, they're not prepared for lawyer fees and bail. I don't say shit just to be saying it. It's a reason behind everything." He said as Felicia came out of the bathroom.

"You okay gurl?" Ronnie asked her.

"Yeah gurl. I'm good. It was just a misunderstanding but we straight now. Ain't that right, Boo?" Felicia said winking her eye at Ramon.

"Yeah we good, Felicia." Ramon said dryly.

"Fat, we got a meeting tomorrow." Ronnie and Felicia masked up and put a 6 on the dope. "Oh, and y'all know the drill." Ramon said as both women began to strip naked and go to work on cutting the dope.

Chapter 10

As Fat Man entered the basement of the house on Lenmore Street, he found Stank in the chair sleep.

"Wake the fuck up Nigga! Ain't no sleep jumpin' off." Fat Man said waking Stank up.

"Wus up? Did everything check out?" Stank said half sleep.

"Yeah, it's all correct so we 'bout to let you go. Hey Liz, come down here." Fat Man called upstairs.

Liz came down the steps in a red teddy making her shapely body sexier than the body dressed she often wore ever could.

"Yeah babe, wus up?" She said eyeing the crotch of Stank as he instantly got aroused.

"Ramon said for you to take care of 'ole boy real good. I got your bus ticket upstairs." Fat Man said speaking to both as he untied Stank.

I wonder if I could get the drop on this nigga, Stank thought as Fat Man was untying his feet. Fat Man felt the vibe as soon as he was about to untie his left arm.

"On second thought, Liz un-tie this fool and if you try something crazy, give your soul to God because your ass belong to me," Fat Man said pulling out his pistol and pointing it at Stank as Liz untied him.

"Nawl, it ain't like that man." Stank said lying through his teeth. As soon as he was free, he tried to stand and fell straight on his face.

"Damn, my legs are sleep," Stank said from the floor.

"Well, wake them up." Fat Man stood over top him.

"Can I get a hand?" Stank asked as he tried to get his legs up under him.

"Liz," Fat Man motioned for her to assist him with a nod.

She quickly ran over to help him off the floor.

"Whew!" Liz said smelling the foul stench that had infested his body for the last few days made her face frown.

"Clean him up and take care of him real nice." Fat Man winked his eye at Liz as she struggled to get him up the stairs. She remembered when times were much easier. Catch a few tricks and lay under Mouse all day. Now she couldn't afford such a luxury but it beat being broke, she thought as she examined Stank to see if she had to work hard. She was disappointed in his package but she was well versed in how to make a man feel pleasure.

She turned on the shower while helping him into the tub.

"Mama got you now." She said as Stank braced himself against the wall inside the shower. Liz bathed him from head to toe stroking his manhood a few times to keep him up. Stank had thoughts of revenge and pleasure all in his mind as the shower water ran all over his body

"This feels so good," Stank said under the water.

"You ain't felt nothing yet," Liz said smiling up at him removing her wet teddy and revealing her well defined body naked. Stank watched her closely as he suddenly regain full strength. As soon as Liz stepped into the shower, he turned around and entered her from behind forcefully.

"Yeah Daddy! Give it to me rough!" Liz said as she felt his manhood stabbing her womb. Stank looked around the bathroom for an escape route or a weapon but it was no use. The window over the tub was nailed down to the sill and there was nothing to use as a weapon but a plastic comb. *Damn!* He cursed to himself.

"It feels good don't it babe? Mama knows. Oh yeah keep it right there." Liz said faking like she was into it. She just wished he pop off and get it over with.

Stank sped up the pace of his stokes as her moans became louder. Fat Man stood outside the doorway smoking a cigarette listening to the whole thing.

"Oh you nasty whore! Take it you nasty slut!," he loudly stated as he felt the tension in his testicles tighten. Liz was glad it was nearly over.

"Oh cum for Mama, babe. That's right! Fuck me like a dog. You know how I like it. Oh...Mmm...Oh!" She kept faking and throwing her hips back to meet his. She could tell he was near. As soon as she felt the first explosion of his ejaculation, she tightened her pussy muscles like vice grips locking him inside of her.

Stank let out a soft whimper at the feeling of her swallowing him inside her. He shot all of himself into her as she drained him dry. He fell against the wall as she released him from her grasp.

"Alright baby boy. You got a bus to catch. So pull it together." Fat Man said while making a mental note to taste Liz the first chance he got.

"Hold up, man. Let me catch my breath," Stank said as he struggled to regain his senses.

"Look, we got you a ride waiting for you outside, so you got to hurry up." Fat Man went on to say as Liz stepped out of the tub. She turned back to Stank.

"Thanks Tiger. I needed that!" She then winked her eye at him.

Turning to Fat Man, she rolled her eyes in disgust. Soon as she walked past Fat Man, he looked at her big brown sexy ass walk down the hallway to the closet to grab a towel.

"Stop looking at my ass, boy." She said without even turning around.

Stank dried off and got dressed.

"Come on shawty." Fat Man said as they headed out the hallway towards the front door.

"A'ight man, damn!" Stank said as he opened the front door. He then felt a budge in his lower back. Walk slow!," Fat Man commanded as Liz got up and closed the door behind them.

Boo Boo was waiting outside in a parked car directly in front of the house.

"Get in the front." Fat Man ordered as he reached around Stank and opened up the front door on the passenger side.

"Come on man." Boo Boo said as he pointed his gun at Stank covering him while Fat Man was inside the car. Boo Boo started the car and reached for a joint he had rolled previously in the ashtray.

"You wanna hit this man?" He asked Stank as he lit it. The scent of the weed let everyone in the car know it was the truth.

"Hell yeah," Stank responded reaching for the jay.

As soon as he hit it, he felt the rush causing him to get a lil relaxed.

"That's some good shit." Stank said exhaling leaning his head back on the head rest. Fat Man reached over the seat with a wire chocker in the shape of a noose to his crossed arms catching Stank around his Adam's apple. Pulling back with all his might, he began to strangle him.

Stank grabbed for the wire but wasn't able to get his fingers in between his throat and the wire. He continued to struggle as he felt the air in his lungs but just couldn't exhale. The more he struggled, the harder Fat Man pulled on the choker. He even placed a knee in the back of Stank's seat to gain more leverage.

Stank kicked at the dashboard violently trying to get away from the choke hold, but it was no use. He felt the life slipping out of him little by little as blood started to fill his eyes and his skin started to turn purple.

Stank's body fell limp as he tried desperately to fight his killer off to no avail. His arms got heavier and his fingers slipped slowly away from the choker. In less than 60 seconds, he fought what seemed like eternity.

His legs spasm one last time in a lost effort and his entire frame went limp and his bowels released.

"Damn shawty, you ain't say the nigga was gon shit on himself." Boo Boo said covering his face with one of his hands.

"I ain't know he was gone shit in his pants either. So shut the fuck up and drive." Fat Man said as he released the choker and leaned back in the seat.

Boo Boo drove a short distance to 2908 Apartments on Jefferson Davis Hwy and pulled up around the back.

"You sure this joint vacant?" Fat Man asked as he opened the door to get out.

"If it wasn't, I wouldn't have brought no dead ass shitty body down here." Boo Boo said as he helped Fat Man with the body.

Detective Howard was awakened by the phone.

"Hello," he said answering the phone looking at the clock on the night stand.

"Well, you'll never guess who just popped up?" Det. Hutch said looking down on the dead body as he spoke over the radio.

"Who?" Det. asked sounding half asleep.

"Ya boy Stank." Det. Hutch responded.

"Where at? Goes Det. Howard now sitting up in the bed.

"2908 on J.D. dead as a door knob," Hutch went on to express.

"Is everything alright babe?" Felicia said rolling over.

"Yeah, I gotta go to work. Lock up when you leave." Howard stated as he quickly got dressed and exited out the bedroom.

As soon as she heard the car start up and leave, she picked up the phone and dialed a number.

"Put Ramon on the phone Connie. It's important." Felicia said while playing with the telephone cord.

"What happened?" Howard said to his partner as he greeted him as he got out the car.

"Strangled by a wire choker or something of that nature, Hutch responded as they both looked over the crime scene.

"I presume it's clean," Goes Howard.

"Clean as a bottle of Pine Sol." Hutch responded.

"Any witnesses?" Howard asked looking at the crowd of nosey spectators.

"I wish but it's one thing I do know, whoever killed him didn't do it here," Said Hutch, as they walked into the vacant apartment.

"The victim has restraint marks on his wrist and ankles. Couple that with the fact it's a trail of his bowel from the parking lot to this area here." Hutch goes on to state while pointing at the ground with his ink pen.

"So, what do you think? Same people from Jefferson Village?" Howard asked.

"It gotta be," Hutch responded looking around to make sure nobody was earshot.

"That's Mouse's nephew, right?" He whispered to Howard.

"Yeah, it's been a bad week for the Jones Family." He whispered back.

"Not so good for us either. The Chief and Mayor are all over us." Hutch kept looking at the crime scene.

"Well, that's the least of our problems. We got to answer to the people up top for that Market incident as well." Howard walked around the scene, too being careful not to contaminate the crime scene.

"Get the Crime Scene Investigators on the down here and let them do what they do, then file the report and notify the family." Howard stated as he exited the apartment to smoke a cigarette.

"This ain't adding up. These muthafuckas droppin' like flies and the powers have been breathing down our necks along with the Commission. I swore to uphold the law but now I've taken a backseat to justice for some money; the root of all evil. I've got to find a way to reclaim my soul from the devil and right this wrong." He says to himself.

"You good over there?" Hutch asked.

"Yeah, I was just thinking about some things." He replied.

"I can tell. What's her name and does she have a sister?" Hutch burst out laughing.

"Nah, it ain't a female. It's deeper than that."

"But ain't you married?" Howard said looking at this partner with a shameful look.

"Man, you know I am but I like to sample other treats from time to time." Hutch said.

"Well, look here. I got somewhere to be at 12noon tomorrow so meet me early in the morning around 6am so we can take care of the paperwork and notify the family. Get them to do an I.D. for the body and get something on our stomachs before we go, holler at our people." Howard said as he opened the door to his car.

"Well, it's almost 6 now so where you headed?" Hutch asked him.

"I left a house guest unattended to and she's a strange bed fellow." Howard said laughing as he shut the door to his car and pulled off. Only if he knew how stranger she really was.

Chapter 11

At 9:45am, Ramon left out of his mother's house in Blackwell on 12th street.

"You are going to meet that bitch," Connie said stepping onto the front porch behind him.

"What bitch?" he asked.

"Don't play stupid with me." She immediately rolled her eyes at him with her arms folded across breast and turned her head to look up the street.

"Look, I ain't got time for this right now." He said as he turned to walk away.

"I know what happened the other day. She calling you Boo now." She said with her words stopping Ramon dead in his tracks.

"Listen," he said turning around and walking towards her.

"Felicia is just part of the team and I'm the coach. I tell her the plays I draw, she executes them. Did I fuck her? No! But she's my go to player right now. So I have to let her have her way or she gonna try to find a different team." He stated as she suddenly cut him off.

"I'll play her position and mine." Connie said. "Fire that bitch or I will."

Ramon chuckled. "Oh you think you can fill her shoes, huh?" He asked knowing what her answer would be.

"Hell yeah! What can that bitch do that I can't?" she asked with tears in her eyes.

"You don't wanna go there. Trust me." He said.

"Let's go there." She challenged him while pushing him in his chest.

"All the shit I do for you and you gone treat me like I ain't shit." She said pushing him again.

"Look it's like this. You don't realize the depth of this shit so I'll explain but first calm down." He then grabbed both her arms softly.

"Felicia is a street girl and you're not. She got a spot to stash the work. The same work she will get arrested for if the people kick in her shit. While I run these streets, she holds the fort down. You get all of my free time and spend a lot of the money we, meaning the team make. Of course, she wants me because she wants to be you, but she can't be you, not with me. Nor can you be her while you're with me. You keep saying I fucked her but I didn't. She gave me some head. I was caught up in the moment. She throws herself at me every chance she gets and if I didn't let her, at least have some part of me, I would eventually have to kill her because she knows too much. But that will never happen." He said.

"I'm gone kill that bitch! I told you..." she said as she started to cry. "I hate you! I hate your no good ass!" She pulled away from him.

"Boo listen," he said as he grabbed her arms again.

"Get your hands off me. Don't touch me muthafucker." She said trying to pull away from him.

"Look, it's like this. I'm in love with you and you are the one I want to share my world with but as long as I'm in the game, I have to share my world with Felicia or someone that's like her or maybe even worst. So if you can't understand this, then you really don't understand us or our relationship." Ramon said releasing her arms and kissing her softly on the lips.

"I gotta go meet someone very important and it's not her. Trust me on this." He said.

"You know what Ramon, I'm gonna let a nigga eat my pussy and see how you feel when you find out." She said.

"Well, if that'll make you happy then do that. We'll be even. Yet, you gotta at least tell the nigga that was his last meal." He said as he ran to the car and left. It was 9:55am.

When Ramon pulled into the parking lot of Glenn's Diner, Fat Man was already in position. As soon as Ramon had parked, he walked over to meet him.

"Damn dog, it's not like you to be late. I was starting to get a lil worried." Fat Man said to Ramon eyeing him closely for any signs of nervousness.

"Nah, I had to straighten Connie before I left. It took a lil longer than usual." Ramon said as he turned to face his partner.

"You ready to go claim what's ours." Fat Man asked with a sly grin on his face.

"Ready as I'll ever be." Ramon said as they both headed for the Diner.

As soon as they entered, they saw Boo Boo and Ski Bo in the booth closet to the bathroom. Other than that, it was basically empty.

"Have a seat." They heard a female voice say from behind.

"Your party has gone to the restroom." They turned around to see a young white waitress with short blonde hair smiling at them.

"Okay, where are we sitting?" Ramon asked smiling back at her.

"Right over there." She said pointing at the booth in the corner furthest away from the window. She escorted then to their seats and handed them two menus.

"Excuse me Ms. Doris," Ramon said reading her name tag, "how many people are with this party?"

"One other person I think he seen you when you pulled up and he reserved this booth over here. Is there a problem with your seat?" She asked.

"No. Everything is fine." Fat Man said

"We'll call you when we're ready to order." He continued.

"Alrightee then," she said walking away to go tend to Boo Boo and Ski Bo.

"Man, I thought we were meeting that old white broad." Fat Man said taking his seat across from Ramon so they can watch each other's backs.

"It's probably that same clown from Woodfolks; if so, we're out of here." Ramon responded as a heavy build tall clean cut black man came from the restroom towards them.

"Damn, he looks familiar." Ramon said low enough for only Fat Man to hear as he approached.

"Morning gentleman," Tank said to them both.

"Well, I'll be damn," Fat Man said all excited.

"Man, I know who you are?" Fat Man said excitedly. "Ramon, you don't know who this is? Man you were my hero growing up." As Fat Man jumped up and gave Tank a firm hand shake.

"Have a seat man." Fat Man acted like he was a small kid again.

"Thank you very much but I'd like to get down to business." Tank said taking his seat. He hated attention.

"So, you're Ramon, Jr., huh?" My name is Tank Williams." He politely introduced himself.

"I thought you looked familiar, but how did you go from there to here?" Ramon casted a confused look on his face.

"It's a long story but we'll save that for another day. I don't have much time so let's get down to business. I mean if that's what you're here for." Tank said as he picked up a menu.

"Cool with me." Ramon responded

"First, I want to discuss payment for the shipment you stole from me. You have incurred the debt of your fore-fathers as well. So the way I see it, you owe us about 1.5 million dollars. "Tank said not even looking up from the menu.

"1.5 million? You using some of that shit or what?" Ramon said laughing at his comment.

"No. Actually it's a lot more than that, but I'd rather cut some of the expenditures allocated from other revenues acquired from your actions, which you're solely responsible." Tank, matter of factly stated, placing the menu back down on the table.

"Come again." Ramon tilted his head lowering one eye.

"Oh, you're not familiar with accounting? Let me come down to your dumb level. You've caused a lot of monetary damage to our organization with your guerilla tactics and methods of war. Therefore, instead of making you pay for the rest of the cost of the damage, you'll just pay us for the product and keep the rest of the money as a bonus." Tank said, as he motioned for the waitress to come over.

"Are you ready to order?" she asked.

"Let me get four scrambled eggs, a rib eyed steak, lightly toasted white bread, some grape jelly, and a large orange juice." Tank said.

"And you fellas?" She asked still writing Tank's order down on her pad.

"Nothing for us," Ramon says.

"You know breakfast is the most important meal of the day." Tank said with a sly grin. "Come on. I insist." He added.

"Coffee, two creams, one sugar and a Danish." Ramon said looking down on the menu.

"Will that be cheese or apple, sir."

"Cheese," Ramon responded.

"And you sir?" She asked Fat Man while writing on her pad.

"The same as him," Fat Man answered nodding towards Ramon.

"Four scrambled eggs, a rib eyed steak, lightly toasted white bread, some grape jelly, and a large orange juice for you." She stated motioning to Tank.

Two coffees, one sugar, two creams in each and two cheese Danishes. Separate bills? She asked reading their order back.

"No all on one bill." My treat, Tank said.

"It'll be right up," she said.

"Thank you," Tank said.

"You're welcome," she said as she headed off to the kitchen.

"Service with a smile, I wish all business was that simple." Tank said looking directly at Ramon.

"Look here Tank, this ain't football. You're playing by a different set of rules." Ramon said gritting on Tank.

"A different set of rules, yes, but rules nonetheless. It has to be order or the game is unorganized. Dudes in the sandlot league don't get paid like professionals. So which are you?" Tank said to Ramon.

"Fat Man, excuse us for a minute," Ramon said glaring at Tank from across the table.

"Yeah go join your ear hustling homeboys over there." Tank said pointing to Boo Boo and Ski Bo without ever looking up. As soon as Fat Man, left he let Tank have it.

"I'm not trying to disrespect you or anything like that but what's done is done. I got your shit and it's moving like hot cakes. Please know, ain't nothing soft about me or my team. On the field you was the man. Even with blockers in front of you, they still got your ass. They did it in sports, I did it in the streets. So don't talk down to me like you can't get got because you can," Ramon said.

"And I guess you can't get got, huh? Tank replied with a sly grin.

"You here now and if I give the word, everybody in here dying that ain't playing on our side." Ramon said placing his hand inside of his jacket, as the rest of his team did the same.

"I know you're a cold blooded killer, that's why I informed my team of who I was meeting with and my team got a lot of influence because they are the law, which makes me above the law, so to speak." Tank said holding up his hand to cut the conversation short as Doris returned with their orders.

"Here you gentlemen are", she said placing the food on the table, "

"Will that be all?"

"Yes, that'll be all," Ramon said.

"Alrightee then, she said rippin the tab from her pad, placing it on the table and walking away.

"This looks delightful." Tank said picking up his fork and digging into his scrambled eggs.

"As I was saying, Ramon you're playing with the big boys, I like your spunk and all but you don't have no business savvy. So this is what I'm gone do, I'm going to wipe away your debt of 1.5 million in part for now. The money was and still is a bonus.

That will be recouped. My bad, repaid on the third shipment. Instead of looking at it, like you stole or high jacked our shipment, you just received it all on consignment which will be repaid on this shipment and the next unless you can come up with one million dollars off this shipment." Tank said looking across at Ramon.

"That's not gone work because my team gotta eat." Ramon said.

"Nah, that's off your cut. So I figure minus living expenses, you should pay this off in a matter of say, three months. Being that you're able to move the entire product you just got on your own. That's where you'll start at." Tank said as he started to eat again.

"What about that white bitch? What's her roll?" Ramon asked as he sipped his coffee.

"She's just a front for our operation that was your father's idea. I have to admit, your father was a genius when it came to moving drugs. The best this organization has ever had the pleasure of working with. His untimely demise came from business with pleasure. She's nothing more than a pawn on this big ass chest board and my advice to you is to let it ride and swallow your pride on this one. I'll handle all dealings with her." Tank said taking a sip from his glass of orange juice.

"So, what about the list?" Ramon asked.

"It's yours to use as you wish. That was solely you father's idea. It's coded, but I'm sure you can decipher the code. You do know how to decipher the code, right?" Tank said looking half way up at Ramon from his plate of food. Before Ramon could answer, "you don't know that you got. Do you?" He asked as Ramon held his head down.

"All you have to do is think of the political figures that run the state and their biggest contributors. Your father knew and met a lot of these people through Jane. Everybody is dirty from the Mayor to the Chief of Police. The only names that are not on there is people in our organization, and presume those names will never be spoken." Tank said, searching Ramon's eyes for an answer and then continued on. "Well, then I'll need one last commitment from you and that's just as important as all of the rest." Tank took his napkin to wipe his mouth.

"What's that?" Ramon asked biting a piece of his Danish.

"No more killing. You're good at what you do, but it brings a lot of heat on us. The Jefferson Village thing was effective but too sloppy. Stank's was perfect. Even though we were able to let the heat cool off, it cost us as well. You'll have freedom regain over your area. Just no more bodies; not now, and you clear every move in that regard with me before you make it. If you don't, I'll take that as a sign of disrespect and treat it as such. Can you agree to these terms?" Tank asked extending his hand to Ramon.

"Yeah, that ain't a problem, but what about self-defense?" Ramon asked holding his hand slightly back from Tanks grasp.

"Understandable, but any calculated moves have to be done on my order alone. Do we have a deal?" Tank said, with his hand still extended.

"Yes, we do," Ramon said shaking his hand. "I take it that those are your most trusted men?" Tank said, acknowledging the other guys.

"Yeah, fo-sho!" Ramon said looking in their direction.

"Good, I don't ever want them to know when we're meeting again nor do I ever what to see them again. I'll meet Fat Man only if anything ever happens to you." Tank said wiping his mouth with the napkin.

"Now if there is no further business to discuss this meeting is adjourned. I have other matters to tend to; however, it's been a pleasure and I look forward to doing business with you. Now, if you'll excuse me, I have another client that will be here shortly," Tank said, shaking Ramon's hand again and motioning him to leave the diner.

As Ramon got up to leave, he motioned for the rest of the guys to follow suit. Fat Man stopped by the table and got the Danish he ordered.

"Holla at you Tank," he said taking a big bite from the Danish and walking out the diner.

"You greedy as motherfucker," Boo Boo said as they walked to their cars.

"Shit I ain't ate shit all day nigga. It's damn near noon." Fat Man said stuffing the rest of the Danish in his mouth.

"Oh shit, what the fuck is she doing here?" Ramon said as Felicia pulled into the parking lot with her new Caddy.

"Wus up Boo?" She said to Ramon rolling down her window.

"Wus up?" Ramon said.

"I thought that was your car, I need to holler at you Ramon," she said opening up her car door.

"Not right now, go home and I'll call you" Ramon said trying to get away from the diner.

"Hell naw! I ain't gone keep being put on hold. So either you ride with me or I'll park and ride with you." She snapped trying to show off. Ramon had to let her win.

"Ride with me. Boo Boo, take her car." Ramon said.

"Oh hell naw. Boo Boo, you drive Fat Man's car and Fat, you drive mine." She said getting out of her car and running over to Ramon's car.

"Just do it and let's go." One by one they left the parking lot with Ramon leading the way and Fat Man bringing up the rear.

As soon as Fat Man was pulling out, an unmarked police car was pulling in.

"Bitch." Howard said, as he was pulling in.

"Wus up Partner?" Hutch said.

"It's nothing. I got to handle this on my own." He said as he watched the car of his lover ride off into the sunset.

Chapter 12

In the basement of the house on Lenmore, all you could hear was the money flipping through the electronic money counter.

"How much you got there?" Ramon asked Fat Man as he placed a stack of money on the table that looked like thousands of stacks.

"1.25 million dollars over here," he answered with a smile on his face. It had only been a week since they stepped on the dope they had stolen from the Market.

"That's the overall collection or do we have more in the street?" Ramon asked, while wrapping each stack in rubber bands.

"Nah," he said looking at a piece of paper. "Jackson Ward boys still unaccounted along with your guys from Tidewater." Fat Man didn't like networking out of town but it was no way they could move all that heroin in Richmond, especially when damn near everybody had the same connect.

"Look here shawty," Ramon said to Fat Man, "it's time to treat ourselves and the team. Everybody been doing so good it's time to celebrate our arrival. You, dig?"

"Fo' sho! But we still got these outstanding debts. So what about them?"

"Send Ski Bo over to the Jackson Ward, then we'll send Ray, Hank, and Liz to collect with the Tidewater Boys.

Detective Howard turned up his bottle as he started his engine and followed the love of his life from a moderate distance.

When Felicia pulled up in front of The Ebony Island Night Club, it was packed. She stopped over thirty times in the parking lot to let people past as they headed to the club's entrance. She found a parking space on the far side of the parking lot and backed her car in.

Getting out, she noticed that it was nothing but Lincolns, Cadillacs, and Ninety-eights. But she was a better ride then anything in the parking lot as she strolled across with a red satin body fitting dress on with black fishnet stockings that complimented her Italian leather handcrafted six inch pumps, that made her ass sit higher than normal. The gold necklace had a half karat diamond encrusted crown with the word "*Queen*" right under it. The black mink shawl draped over her shoulders only added more class to her air of royalty.

She felt the glaring eyes of both sexes as she backed stroked in the attention. Admirable and desirable energy flowed all the way to the door where the line traveled around the block. It was no way she was going to stand in that long line and especially not in the back of it. She walked to the front of the line.

"Yo shawty, the line is that way." She heard a slim fella of fair skin complexion say that set off other negative objections to her intrudence.

"Hey you can't do it like that Miss Lady." The 6'5" muscle bound bouncer said as she stepped to the front.

"You don't expect me to wait for this line to go down, I know." Felicia said shooting him a flirtation smile.

"I wish I could let you by these people but I can't make any exceptions." He said.

"Not even for me?" Opening up her shawl to reveal a lengthy amount of cleavage revealing her pendant and making his mouth water like a fountain.

"I'm sorry but I ..." He was cut off from behind

"What's going on Big Man?" Fat Man said coming out the club.

"This young lady here..." he was cut off again.

"Felicia, girl come on in here. Why you waiting outside." Fat Man said pulling her by the arm.

"I was trying to get in, but he was holding me up." She said walking pass the bouncer.

"I'm sorry," said the bouncer. "I didn't..." he was drowned out by the loud music and the crowd of people inside of the club. Speaking over the music she asked

"Where Ramon and them at?"

"We got a table over there by the dance floor." Fat Man said as they climbed the little flight of steps pointing to his left.

"What are you drinking?" he said leading her to the bar.

"Coke and rum," she replied as they made their way through the crowd of people straight ahead to the bar.

"What'll it be?" the bartender said while wiping the counter top of the bar with a hand towel.

"Give me 10 bottles of Dom and one rum and coke." Fat Man said pulling out a knot of one hundred dollar bills.

"That'll be one thousand, five hundred, two dollars and fifty cent," the bartender said while undressing Felicia with his eyes. Fat Man handed him sixteen one hundred dollar bills and said,

"Deliver it to the table and keep the change."

"Hell man, I'll take the rum and coke now," Felicia said smiling at him.

"Okay give me the mixed drink now, and send the rest of the bottles over." Fat Man said looking at Felicia smiling back. With her drink in hand they headed back towards the entrance as many faces in the crowd acknowledged their presence, some with head nods, others with pounds. A lot of the men in the club winked eyes at Felicia as she walked past, but her eyes belonged to one man and it wasn't the one on her arm. As they made the turn to go to the table they saw a camera flashing from the picture booth. As soon as they got near the booth, they had seen their team flicking it up and showing off. As soon as Ramon spotted them he waved for them to come over.

"Hold up, hold up. Wait for my peoples." Ramon said to the camera man as Fat Man and Felicia made their way through the crowd. As soon as Felicia saw Connie her mood was quickly dampened.

"Oh hell naw bitch, you ain't getting in this picture." Connie snapped as she approached Felicia.

"Girl please, and I know it's past your curfew, do your mom's know you're up in here." Felicia said dropping her purse getting on the defense.

"Hell naw, we ain't gon start this shit." Ramon said pulling Connie back before she could get in striking distance.

"Just keep that bitch on a long leash." Connie said to Ramon while gritting on Felicia.

"No matter how long the leash is, when the bitch is in heat, the top dog is usually the one to fuck her anyway." Felicia said smiling at Connie kneeling down to get her purse.

"This is not the time nor the place for any of this bullshit. We're here to have fun." Ramon said as he gave Fat Man a pound.

"Come on camera man do your job," Fat Man said hugging Felicia and pulling her away from Ramon and Connie. Ramon started tossing money up in the sky as the camera flashed away. Every member of his team got a chance to be in the picture. Boo Boo, Ski Bo and even Liz made it back from Tidewater along with the lower levels of the team to attend this affair, as the camera flashed away. The bottles had arrived to the table in ice buckets along with champagne glasses.

Liz picked the money up with the two shopping bags she got from the corner. When the camera man brought the pictures to the table, Ramon handed him a hundred dollar bill. When everyone got to the table, Ramon and Fat Man popped the corks of 3 bottles and started pouring everyone glasses.

"A toast..." Ramon said holding up his glass, "to success, less stress, no arrest, and for being the best."

"Here here!" everyone at the table responded. All eyes were on Ramon and his team as they partied for most the night dancing and drinking expensive labels of fine wine.

"Man this is the life." Fat Man said to Ramon.

"Yea, we worked hard for all we have. So why not enjoy the profits of our labor." He said taking a sip from his glass. Felicia had been waiting all night for this moment as she seen Connie kiss Ramon on the cheek and head for the lady's room. Besides the rum and coke from earlier that night she had one glass of wine, while everyone else drank like they was dying of thirst including Connie. As soon as Connie was out of sight she pounced on her prey.

"Come on boo," she said grabbing Ramon's arm.

"We haven't danced all night." Guiding Ramon to the dance floor as fate would have it. Heat Wave came blaring through the speakers as the DJ said, "Let's slow it down a bit."

"Always and forever, each moment with you..." Felicia sang along with the record in Ramon's ear as they slow danced on the floor.

"You know you need to cut this shit out you doing." Ramon said in her ear as they danced.

"You need to put the baby in her crib for tonight and come to my room till dawn." Felicia said sucking on Ramon's ear lobe.

"You just don't stop it do you." He said as he felt the bulge in his pants stiffen.

"I can tell you don't really want me to stop." She said letting him know she felt him as well. The song ended and Ramon pulled away from her.

"Where you going?" she asked.

"I got to get back before Connie comes out." He said

"To late for that," she said looking over Ramon's shoulder she had seen her since the second verse of the song. Connie was blood warm as they walked back to the table together.

"Bitch what I told you." Connie said slipping her high heels off.

"Connie I done told you to chill; we weren't doing nothing but dancing." Ramon said as he stood between the two of them.

"Why you had to wait till I left before you had your dance then?" She asked trying to kill Felicia with her eyes.

"So immature," Felicia said stepping around the table to avoid her reach.

"Oh yeah, Ramon I got something for you." Felicia said reaching into her purse.

"A little something I picked up. I hope you like it." Pulling out a jewelry box, Ramon looked down at the box as she placed in his hands.

"Go head open it." She insisted.

"Thanks," Ramon said not really wanting to open it in front of Connie.

"Come on I'm waiting" she said.

Against his better judgment, he opened the box and was pleased at what was inside.

"Oh shit, this is fly as hell." He said removing the 14 karat gold necklace with the one karat diamond encrusted crown with the word king under it.

"Put it on," she insisted grabbing the necklace from the box and placing it around his neck.

"This calls for a picture right here." She said leading him to the picture booth.

Ramon looked back at Connie, "Chill boo, we'll be right back." He said as he stepped away and sat his glass on the table.

Connie had seen enough as she grabbed her coat and headed off for the door but she had to walk past the booth to leave. As they were ready to pose for the picture Ramon made sure the necklace was in full view.

"Hold up," Felicia said

"We got to do this one night," and for the first time that night, she removed her black mink shawl and revealed the total package of the blood red satin dress with the open back and shoe string straps that tied a bow tie knot around the back of her neck.

When she turned around Ramon saw the necklace as she walked towards him. "Oh so you think you got all of the sense huh?" he said smiling at her.

He had to admit she did look fine as hell tonight and the necklace only added to her sex appeal. As they posed for the picture, Connie walked up. Seeing them together wasn't enough to turn her stomach but when she saw the matching necklaces she could've hit the roof. As soon as Ramon's focus came back from the flash of the camera his eyes met Connie's. The pain was evident from the tears streaming down her cheeks, as she turned and hurried out the club.

"Hold up." Ramon said pushing Felicia aside as he chased behind Connie.

Seeing Ramon leaving from afar Fat Man ran over to Felicia.

"Wus up with Ramon?" he asked noticing the necklace around her neck.

"He gone after his lil girl. I guess he's going to make sure she gets home alright." She said waiting on her picture to develop.

"Come on." He said pulling her by the arm.

"What about my picture and my show wait a minute," She screamed.

"It'll be here when you get back you're going to apologize." When they got outside Ramon and Connie were talking by his car.

"Excuse me Connie, Felicia has something she would like to say to you." Fat Man said leading her face to Connie and Ramon.

"Ramon, I'm sorry for dancing with you without Connie's permission." She said smacking her lips.

"And Connie, I'm sorry for making you upset, but most of all I apologize for you not being half the woman I am, but it's not your fault you can't help that you was born to be inferior." Felicia said smiling at her.

Connie swung on her and missed, but landed a kick to her stomach with the point of one of her pumps, making Felicia fold over in pain.

"SMACK!" Connie caught her opened hand across her left cheek causing her to fall over.

"Bitch Ima kill your stanky pussy ass." Connie said as she tried to stomp her as Ramon pulled her off her feet.

"Let me go." Connie said trying to break the hold Ramon had on her.

"Fat Man, get Felicia out of here. I told you not to disrespect her no more. I should let her whoop your ass but that'll be too good for you." Ramon said as he struggled to keep the untamed cat in his arms.

Fat Man reached down and helped Felicia to her feet.

"Let that bitch go." Felicia said gathering herself as she got to her feet.

"Oh I got your bitch." Connie shot back.

"Fat Man get her out of here." Ramon said still holding for dear life.

"Come on, Felicia." Fat Man said pulling her by the arm.

Felicia tried to pull away but the grip of a 6'4" 290 muscle bound black man was too much for her 5'5" 135 pound frame.

"That's alright bitch, Ima see you again. After I whoop your ass I'm gone really be the queen of the pack." She said screaming as Fat Man pulled her back towards her car. The caddy stood out amongst all the other cars there due to her thirty day tags. Felicia was still trying to break loose as they got to her car.

"Let me go, just let me go." She huffed and puffed as she fought to no avail.

"That's enough for tonight." Fat Man said trying to get her to cool off; he penned her against the driver's side door.

"I ain't going nowhere without my shit." She said looking him in his face breathing hard.

"Well you just gone have to wait here all night." Fat Man said as he held her in his arms.

Liz walked up with her shawl, purse and picture.

"Here you go girl," Liz said handing her possessions.

"You are a queen for real. She know she ain't got shit on you girl." She continued being phony as hell and laughing on the inside.

"Oh you think you gone leave me, huh?" Detective Howard said as he jumped from the woods.

"What are you doing here?" Felicia asked, caught squarely off guard.

"No, the question is what are you doing here?" he said as he staggered near her and Fat Man.

"Who this?" Fat Man said as he kept himself between Felicia and Det. Howard.

"Nah, muthafucka who you and what you doing with my woman?" Det. Howard said tripping over himself and falling hard against the truck of her car.

"You drunk ass, non fucking, pussy eatin, and small dick having ass muthafucker. I know you didn't just dent my shit." Felicia said as she tried to get around Fat Man.

"Get the fuck off my shit!" she screamed.

"Oh you with your street nigga you don't love me no more." He said trying to pull himself together. Liz slid off to the club to go get Ramon and them.

"Love nigga, I ain't never love your ass." She said leaning back on her car reaching in her purse for a cigarette.

"So this is what you are leaving me for?" Det. Howard said looking at Fat Man.

"Look man you drunk and you need to go home somewhere and sleep it off." Fat Man said as he approached him with his hands extended in front of him.

"Don't touch me you lying motherfucker, I saw you driving her car the other day leaving the diner." Det. Howard said sparking a thought in Fat Man's head as he remembered.

"Oh wow shawty you got it all wrong." Fat Man said

"Wrong my ass, I'm the police I ain't never wrong. He said pulling his pistol out.

"Wus up now, Mr. Dope man? You ain't so tough now are you? Why y'all always gotta take the good ones huh? Why y'all always got to have the best looking ones huh? Tell me Mr. Dope man, why I ain't good enough?" Det. Howard snapped pointing his gun dead at Fat Man's chest.

"You got your people mixed up." Fat Man said slowly backing away keeping his body in between Felicia and the gun.

"No, I don't and I hate all you rotten Muthafuckers." Det. Howard said as tears began to fill his eyes.

"I don't even know you man so..." boom boom boom boom boom all five shots hit him squarely in the chest.

"Nooo!" Felicia yelled as she tried to keep his body from falling to the ground. "Fat Man hold on baby," she cried seeing blood jump out his chest and pour from his back, blood spilled from his mouth as he tried to speak.

"You pussy muthafucka," Ramon said running up with the rest of the team following suit. "boom, boom, boom, boom, boom, boom, pow, pow, pow, pow, gunfire came from everywhere hitting Det. Howard all over his body. As he fell to the ground, Ramon stood over his lifeless body and shot him in the face five times. When he turned around Fat Man was smiling and reaching out for him.

"Hold on shawty, you gone be alright, just hold on." He said trying to comfort his best friend.

"You you you got his bitch ass didn't you?" Fat Man said with blood coming from his mouth.

"Yeah, I got him for you." Ramon said holding his hand.

"Good," Fat Man said nodding his head

"Cause when we get to hell I'm gone kill his ass again." As he turned his face to Felicia he smiled and shook his head.

"Don't cry, I'm gone be alright." He turned to face Connie and said "forgive her, we all make mistakes." Connie just nodded her head. Fat Man smiled and tried to say something else but he couldn't get it out as he coughed and blood came out his mouth. His body shook violently and released one final gasp of air.

"No, aww no." Ramon cried holding Fat Man's hand and burying his face into his bloody chest.

Chapter 13

Ramon was crying when he called his mother's house later that night.

"Hello." Hattie Mae said awaken out of the sleep.

"Mama it's me," he said

"Baby what's wrong?" showing great concern because he never had called his mother so late before.

"Mama, Fat Man is dead," he managed to say trying to fight back his tears.

"Lord, no! Babe what happened?" She said as tears started to fill her eyes. She always looked at Fat Man as one of her own sons. Since him and Ramon started their friendship years ago.

"The police, mama the police." Ramon couldn't get it out...

"Ramon you need to come home baby. I need to see you to know that you're alright." She pleaded as her heart dropped from sensing her son was in danger.

"Mama, I can't they'll come looking for me there," he said.

"For what? What have you done boy?" She said crying. "I can't talk now, but Connie should be there shortly, she'll explain everything. I love you mama and tell Ms. Norma, I'm sorry," he said, as he began to sob. "I'll tell Norma Ramon, but baby come home. I need you to come home." She begged.

"Mama I can't. I love you." He said

"I love you too baby but I need..."click:

"Hello, Ramon, Ramon, oh Lord no Ramon," she yelled into the phone.

"Mama what's wrong." Sandra said running into her bedroom.

"Girl, Johnny low done killed Fat Man," Hattie Mae said crying.

"No, oh God no, not again," Sandra said crying and running into her mother's arms to share the grief. Bing bong, bing bong. They both ran to the door in hopes it was Ramon. When they opened it they saw Connie and Ronnie standing on the porch crying.

Detective Hutch was the first on the scene to find his partner's and Fat Man's bodies.

"Oh hell naw," he said seeing Det. Howard's bullet riddled lifeless body. He looked over Fat Man's body and ran off to his car and popped the trunk, he closed the trunk after he pulled next to Fat Man's body and placed a pistol near his right hand.

"Well at least you get one of these Muthafuckers," Detective Hutch said to his partner's dead frame.

"Anybody see anything? Anybody?" he said into the crowd of people, as other officers arrived at the scene.

"Tape this shit off." He yelled at the uniform cop as he got out the car. News trucks and vans came piling out in hopes of being the first to get the scoop,

"This ain't good." He thought to himself.

"Anybody see anything?" Detective Hutch asked the crowd again. "Yeah, I saw something." One man said standing near the yellow crime scene tape.

"Finally," Detective said in relief.

"We got someone willing to come forth." As he walked over to question him everyone in the crowd tensed up. "What's your name sir?" Detective Hutch asked pulling out his pen and pad.

"Names ain't important." The man said smiling showing four gold teeth.

"Okay, I understand just tell me what you saw." He said prepared to write.

"It's simple really. The guy over there with the cheap JC penny loafers on? You know who he is?" The man asked Detective Hutch.

"Yeah, that's my partner. What happened to him?" he asked.

"His bitch ass got what he deserved." The man said laughing as the crowd erupted in a roar of applause and cheer. Detective Hutch couldn't control himself he stole the man dead in the mouth knocking one of his gold teeth out, as the man fell back into the crowd. Man, what's wrong with you. Y'all think this shit is funny. I'll lock all of y'all ass up fucking with me." Detective Hutch said pulling his gun and cuffs out. As he tried to go under the yellow tape he felt someone pull him back.

"That's enough. Get back over here detective." Turning around he saw the face of the OIC (officer in charge) of the graveyard shift commander hicks.

"But sir." He was cut off.

"But my ass detective, you're already lucky this man doesn't file charges against the department. You've set a bad example for your fellow officers. As of this moment, you are relieved of duty and I'll need your badge and service weapon." Commander Hicks demanded, holding out his hand. Detective Hutch didn't try to argue. He just handed them over.

"One more thing before you go detective.' Commander Hicks pulled him in close so only he could hear.

"You done the right thing it's just the cameras caught it all. Wait for me at the station we have to talk; I'll give you this shit back then." Steppin back from him he then said,

"that'll be all detective, your dismissed." Detective Hutch walked to his car, got in and drove straight to the station to await the arrival of Commander Hicks.

Back at the station commander Hicks called Det. Hutch into the office shortly after he arrived.

"Shut the door and have a seat." He said as he removed his coat and hat, sitting down behind his desk, he grabbed the half of cigar and lit it.

"You know the media is going to be all over this, and the little episode with the civilian is only going to complicate our efforts." Commander Hicks said blowing the smoke in the air.

"Yeah, but I was only acting...off of emotion, I fully understand." Commander Hicks said cutting him off,

"But we have unsolved cases from over a week ago that's still getting coverage. Cases you and Det. Howard, God rest his soul, haven't solved yet." Commander Hicks said eyeing him for any type of reaction.

"You know how it is working homicide. Without witnesses you can't get suspects. No suspects no arrest, so on and so forth." Detective Hutch said as he got up and looked out of the office window that faced the desk area and cubicles for other officers.

"Look detective, I understand how hard investigating these cases can get, but I want to know why you and Det. Howard wasn't together tonight?" he asked

"Excuse me?" Detective Hutch said, turning around.

"Let's not play any games because internal affairs are going to be all over this come morning, meaning all over you and all over me." Commander Hicks said placing the cigar in the ashtray. "I don't understand sir?" Detective Hutch said. "Well let me make you understand. This happened on my shift, on my watch." He said pointing his index finger to his chest. "My ass is in a sling as well. You and your partner were supposed to be on duty, tonight. So why was he not with you or was he?"

Commander Hicks hated calling the integrity of his officers into question, but in this case he had no choice.

"No, we weren't together." Detective Hutch said hanging his head down.

"Then why do I have him on the log sheet for mustard?" Commander Hicks said looking over the clip board on his desk.

"I need answers Hutch, because according to this, he died in the line of duty. Internal Affairs is going to be all over this, I done put too much work into this department and this city to lose it all over something outside of police work. So we need to get our story straight now or the 25 years of service I put in ain't shit." Commander Hicks was interrupted by a knock on the door.

"Come in." the uniformed cop stepped in.

"Excuse me sir, the lab reports you asked for are back." The officer said handing Commander Hicks a manila envelope. "Thank you, Alston. That'll be all for now," he said opening up the package. "Sir, yes sir," turning to Det. Hutch.

"I'm sorry about your partner Hutch." Alston said as he exited out of the office door. "It seems we have a problem here." Commander Hutch said as he read over the paperwork he held.

"What is it sir?" Hutch asked wondering what now.

"It seems that the weapon found on our victim was never discharged, nor did the victim have any gun powder residue on his hands. More importantly Det. Howard's blood alcohol level was 0.7, well above the legal limit, so you need to provide me with some answers and quick." Commander Hicks said placing the paperwork on his desk.

"All I can say is that he wasn't with me, as for the log book, I signed him in because I thought he was coming in, but lately he was out of it. At first I just thought his stress was job related, until tonight I never thought it would go this far." Detective Hutch said as he sat back in his seat.

"So what you're telling me is that you have no idea what else it could be?" he asked.

"No sir." Detective Hutch was lying.

"Have you ever heard of Tank Williams?" Commander Hicks asked. "No sir, I can't say that I have." Detective Hutch lied.

"Well that's who you and Detective Howard moonlighted for and who's drug interest y'all protected for the last few weeks." Commander Hicks said leaning up on his desk.

"Sir I didn't know the person we were working for..." Commander Hicks cut him off

"You mean to tell me a highly decorated officer like yourself that specializes in investigating and solving cases, didn't look into who was behind the set up. You got to be shittin' me. Well since you won't come clean; let me inform you on the developments. We have a Confidential Informant deep within the organization. The Clinton Jones murders all have a prime suspect. We don't have the names of the shooters but we have the name of the mastermind. His name is Ramon Baker Jr. and his second in command was gunned down by your partner. All of which doesn't involve Tank Williams directly according to our source. So I need answers and quick or you can kiss your career goodbye unless you can bring me Ramon Baker Jr. dead or alive." Commander Hicks reached for his coat pocket to retrieve Detective's Hutch's badge and gun sliding them across the desk, he said,

"I can keep IA off your back for 72 hours, after that it's out of my hands, and the next time I hear from you, I want to hear that Ramon Baker Jr. is in custody or in a body bag. The choice is yours. But you got 72 hours, now get out of here."

"Thanks sir." Detective Hutch said, as he grabbed his tools of his trade and left the office. Once he was gone, Commander Hicks picked up the phone.

"Tell big boy we bout to kill two birds with one stone." Commander Hicks said. "We knew we could count on you." Leo said hanging up the phone.

"You know they looking for you, they been over the house twice already and I think they're outside now." She said fighting back her tears. "I figured that, but don't worry, I got a trick up my sleeve," he said

"Boy you sound just like your father." She said reminded of how he often laughed in the face of danger. "What daddy got to do with this?" he asked.

"Everything! So listen here and listen good. They killed your father and one of my boys, I'd be damned if I lose you, too. I'd rather visit you in prison for the rest of my life than bury you before you bury me. So turn yourself in." She couldn't believe the words herself, but a locked up child beats having a dead child any day.

"Mama, do you know what you're saying?" he couldn't believe his ears. "Babe they gone kill you if you don't. So if you don't do it for yourself, then please do it for me." She started crying, and her tears always melted his cold heart.

"Okay mama, I'm gone turn myself in, but it's a few things I need to wrap up first. After Fat Man's funeral, I'll turn myself in," he said going against his better judgment.

"Boy don't lie to me. Promise,." She demanded.

"I promise!," he said. She listened to see if he was laughing, she was the only woman on earth Ramon couldn't lie to, not without laughing and keeping a straight face. A thought crossed her mind.

"Boy you can't go to his burial they'll be waiting for you." She said fearful they'd kill him at the service.

"Not if they bury him on the same day they bury the pig that killed him." He said knowing the attendance for fellow fallen officers was mandatory for the vast majority of all police officers in the city.

"So you still got that thing I gave you?" he asked.

"You know that I do boy," She said.

"Good, bake me a cake, I'll be over before I go to the station. I love you mama, I got to go." He said "I love you too boy." She said as they blew each other kisses and hung up. Ramon walked across the parking lot towards his hotel room in Rocky Mount, North Carolina. Before he could put his key in the door, he heard a car pull up behind him. As he turned pulling his pistol, "easy cowboy, let's go inside and talk before we go there," Tank said with a smile on his face. Once inside they got right down to business. "Things went too far with Felicia didn't it?" Tank said leaning back in the chair.

"Yeah, I didn't know ole boy was gone be wide open like that." Ramon said sitting on the bed.

"I needed to know if he was trustworthy, that's why I had you put her on him." Tank said.

"Yeah, when Leo called me in on that, I thought it was a trap. But Liz don't lie to me dog." Ramon said, looking down at his hands.

"Well I'm sorry about Fat Man. He was one of the last of a dying breed," Tank said feeling the lost as well.

"Yeah, thanks man." Ramon said without looking up.

"So did you holla at your people downtown yet." Ramon asked.

"Actually, I did speak with Commander Hicks and he informed me of some very unfavorable news," Tank said getting up from his chair with concern on his face.

"Like what?" Ramon asked sitting up on the edge of the bed.

"It seems that Leo has put a hit out on you." Tank said

"What the fuck you mean? Don't he work for you?" Ramon asked, reaching for his pistol. "I thought he did as well but he made this move on his own. Apparently, he feels that if you're out the way I'll be forced to retire and allow him to live in peace. Leo has been trying to walk away for years but the only way to leave, is death or jail, unless you're cut off.

In his case, he's in too deep to just walk away and be cut off. He took it upon himself to display his true nature of selfishness, for that he must be dealt with. Tank said sitting back down in his chair. "There's another matter that demands our immediate attention. Everyone is calling for blood in this one and we must sacrifice a lamb, Tank added.

"What you mean sacrifice a lamb?" Ramon asked looking confused. "I told you before, this is a business and in order to be successful some people have to be unsuccessful. I know you don't care about that cop you all killed, and maybe he had it coming, but once again, it was sloppy. In our line of work, the less blood the better the business. Simply put, someone has to go to jail, so pick who it is." Tank said.

"Snitch, that's what the fuck you're saying? I'll die before I snitch. What the fuck is wrong with you?" Ramon asked getting off the bed walking over to the chair where Tank was sitting.

"Hell naw, I ain't saying snitch. If I felt you wasn't a stand up type guy, I wouldn't want you to be my number two guy." Tank said standing up to face Ramon.

"What do you mean number two?" he asked lighting the last two words he heard linger in his mind.

"Somebody has to go to jail so we can get the heat off us. We gon make sure he's straight in there and that his family is good out here. It's the only way we can continue to do business," Tank said trying to talk some sense into him.

"What about the list?" Ramon asked.

"It'll give you a bit of leverage but they want a conviction for the police officer. Everybody can't look the other way on this one, Ramon," he said studying him for an answer.

"Okay so what if I buck, then what?" he asked weighing his options.

"You broke your word to me. Only in self-defense remember, but I understand so I'm giving you an out." Tank said hoping that he'll take the out.

"Okay I see where we going with this. If I get someone to take the fall we keep it moving, if not then my fate is sealed?" Ramon asked with a grin on his face.

"Basically," Tank responded.

"Okay, I'm going to turn myself in?" Ramon said.

"You can't do that, don't be stupid." Tank pleaded.

"Nah you gone help out." Ramon said looking directly at Tank.

"How is that?" he questioned his logic.

"Well Felicia said ole boy was drunk when he shot Fat Man," Ramon said as he put the plot together.

"Okay and," Tank said; interested where this would lead. "Well if he's drunk on the job, he didn't use sound judgment when he killed Fat Man." Ramon figured.

"What about the gun they found on Fat Man?" Tank asked.

"Wasn't no gun, you think we were dumb enough to leave a gun behind?" Ramon said clearly angry for thinking Tank would question his intelligence.

"That explain why there was no gun powder residue, Detective Hutch planted the gun." Tank said rubbing his chin with his right hand.

"So that's gon get me a decent deal, where I'll do my little time get out and we pick up where we left off." Ramon said, waiting for Tank to approve. Are you sure you want to go to prison?" Tank asked.

"Yeah, if we can pull it off." Ramon said.

"Pulling it off isn't an issue, I just want you to understand what you're about to do," Tank said looking at him with the utmost admiration.

"So when you think it'll be done?" Ramon asked. "As soon as I talk to the people and you're ready to go." Tank said showing pure confidence.

"Wait until after we bury Fat Man." Ramon said. "Say no more. Oh, I almost forgot," Tank said snapping his fingers.

"I got Leo tied up in the trunk of the car. You know of any dark areas nearby where we can drop him off?" Tank said with a sly grin on his face.

"Do I?" Ramon said, as dirt roads and swallow creeks filled up his mind.

Ramon and Tank drove to a local hardware store to pick up some tools.

"Go inside and get what we need. I have to make a call to Commander Hicks," Tank said as they got out of the car.

"Cool I won't be long." Ramon said as he entered the store. Tank went to the phone and dialed the number to Commander Hicks.

"Hello." Hicks said answering the phone. "Did you stop that yet?" Tank asked. "I can't find him." Hicks said.

"Well you better and I mean soon." Tank said hanging up the phone and waiting outside the store for Ramon. A few minutes later Ramon returned with the tools.

"Did he stop it?" Ramon asked as he loaded the tools into the backseat.

"Nah, but he's working on it." Tank said as they got in the car and drove off.

Commander Hicks put out an A.P.B. (All Point's Bulletin) on Detective Hutch. As he got into his squad car to search for him on his own.

"I got to catch him before he finds Ramon and kills him or gets himself killed. Damn it Leo! Why did I ever let you talk me into this?"

Ramon and Tank pulled up into Sunny Shade Acres at dusk searching for the right spot. They found a nice little patch on the far side of the property. Both men got out the car and began digging a hole. As soon as it was deep enough, they went to get Leo out the trunk of the car.

"Come on here, you bad muthafucka you!" Ramon said as they grabbed his hog tied body and carried him to the hold.

Leo tried to resist but it was no use. His muffled mouth prevented his begging from being heard as he called for help with his terrified teary eyes. Ramon and Tank didn't say a word as they dropped his body in the swallow hole hearing a bone or two pop when he hit the bottom. They just grabbed the shovels and started shoveling the dirt back over top. It took them about 15 minutes to fill the hole back up. They placed the shovels in the trunk and pulled away.

"Do you think somebody will find him here? Tank asked as he lit a cigar.

Ramon eyed him like Tank was crazy.

"Man, who's gonna look for a dead body in a graveyard?" He answered with a grin on his face.

Chapter 14

Detective Hutch sat in a parked car outside of First Baptist Church on Decatur Street in the Blackwell area waiting for Ramon to arrive at Fat Man's funeral.

"Soon as he shows his face, he's a dead man." Hutch thought to himself as the attendance started swelling in front of the church.

Finally, the family cars pulled up.

"Where's Ramon at?" he said out loud to himself as he held the door cracked with his gun cocked and ready. He didn't notice the police cruiser that pulled up behind him.

"Detective Hutch," Officer Alston said walking to his car. Hutch looked back in disgust.

"What are you doing here and what the fuck do you want?" Hutch said stepping out of the car.

"Commander Hicks sent me sir. He said to stand down and go to your partner's funeral. I'm here to escort you." He said looking at his superior officer. He was a wreck.

"Nah, I can't go like this. I can't face his family or members of the department right now. I have to see this through," Hutch said as he kept his eye on the church.

"But Hicks said that if you wasn't there, it would make you look guilty of something..."

"Guilty of what?" Hutch cut him off.

"What? Y'all think I killed my partner?" Y'all got to be crazy. Matter of fact, tell Hicks to kiss my ass and you stay the fuck away from me." Hutch said as he started walking across the street to inspect the cars.

"Where are you going?" Alston asked stepping behind him.

"None of your business. Just tell Hicks you couldn't find me." Hutch said as he looked through the windows of a few cars.

"I can't do that. The C.I. called and said you were here. How do you think I found you?" Alston said trying to convince him to let it go.

"I'm going in and get this muthafucka!"

As he turned around and entered the church doors, he could hear people grieving over the organ chords. The ushers by the door stepped in front of him.

"This is the Lord's house. Weapons aren't allowed in here." Said one of the ushers pointing to the gun he held in his hand. A few people towards the back turned around after hearing that reaching inside of their coats.

"No weapons, huh?" Hutch said placing his gun back in his holster.

"Everybody in here packing for-real." He thought to himself as he pulled out his badge.

"I'm looking for a murder suspect in a major investigation. I'm Detective Hutch of the Richmond Police Department.

"Sir, I don't care who you are," The usher said cutting him off, "there are no guns allowed in this place of worship. You'll have to wait until this service is over. Now I'll ask you to please leave. These people are suffering enough." The usher said.

"Okay, but you're dealing with a very dangerous man." Detective Hutch said placing his badge back in his coat pocket.

"It is not up to me or anyone to judge but the Lord. If the man you're looking for is here, it is my sincere hope that he's here to ask for forgiveness and seek refuge with God. Now

Detective, will you please leave?" The usher said as both of them stepped closer to him.

"Alright I'm gone but don't say I didn't warn you, I'm warning you all." He said, searching the faces in the crowd, he noticed a familiar face. It was the man from the Ebony Island Nite Club he punched in the face smiling at him with a new set of gold teeth.

"I should knock all them thangs out your mouth fool," he said.

As he turned and left, the ushers turned around and nodded to the other ushers that the situation was taken care of. The Pastor turned to the choir and gave the signal for them to be seated as Ramon came walking from behind the choir members and took his seat to Ms. Norma. The Pastor started his eulogy.

When Detective Hutch came down the steps of the church, officer Alston was waiting on him.

"Come on Detective. You're already late," he said, as Hutch walked towards him.

"Let's go. I need to pay my respects," Hutch said getting in his car and pulling off. Officer Alston hit the siren and speeded off to the West End, passing Detective Hutch and leading the way.

As soon as they arrived at the church, they was carrying Detective Howard's casket to the hearse. The news cameras and reports were thick in the crowd of on lookers as Detective Hutch and Officer Alston made their way to join the other officers in attendance.

"Man where have you been?" Sgt. Johnson asked, as he greeted his fellow officer.

"Trying to find Ramon Baker, Jr.," Hutch dryly said, holding his head down and thinking of all the events of the past few months since he and his partner had been receiving dirty money. It wasn't supposed to happen like this he said to himself.

"Yo, I'll help you find the cop killing son of a bitch! Let me holler at some of my informants and I'll get back to you and we'll pick his ass up before dawn." Sgt. Johnson said.

"Alright! That's a bet." Hutch said.

"Excuse me. Aren't you Detective Hutch?" a female's soft voice said from behind.

"Yes, may I help you?" He said turning around to meet her face to face.

"Smack! Smack!"

"That was for leaving him to die like a dog and for not being man enough to show up in time for the service. Come on Patrice." Linda Sue said as they walked off to join their friends.

"Detective Hutch began to feel the water swell in his eyes. Not that the double smack hurt, it was the truth that hurt; a truth so ugly that he was in denial about since a youth. He'd always been a coward. But he'll man up and Ramon's dead body would provide the welcome mat he needed to step up to the plate.

Chapter 15

Felicia was in her apartment watching TV when she heard a knock at the door.

"Who is it?" she said in her soft sexy voice.

"It's Ramon. Open up." He said causing Felicia's pussy to instantly become wet just from hearing his voice. She slid her panties off and hid them under a pillow on the sofa and pulled her T-shirt back down before she ran to open the door.

"Hey Boo," she said as she opened the door and jumped in his arms.

"Wus up girl?" Ramon said as he embraced her kissing her on the cheek.

"I know you can do better than that." She said kissing softly on the lips. A second after their lips met, Ramon turned his head and stepped inside, shutting the door behind him.

"This is not a social call." He said pushing her away trying to get off his urge to rip her insides apart.

"So what's this all about then?" she said clearly showing her disappointment.

"Why you ain't come to Fat Man's funeral?" Ramon asked leaning his back up against the door.

"I didn't want to get into with Connie. Furthermore, I feel bad enough as it is. If I'd never pulled that stunt with Connie, he'll still be here." She said as tears rumbled down her cheeks as she had flashbacks of that deadly night.

"Nah, it's my fault." Ramon said walking over and wiping the tears from her face.

"If I had never put you on that cop, then he wouldn't had been there to begin with." He said taking her into his embrace.

"I'm sorry I put you through that Felicia." He said kissing her gently on the forehead.

"So, now what Ramon?" she said looking in his eyes feeling helpless.

"Now I have to pay the piper, baby girl." He said sitting down on the sofa.

"You don't owe the piper shit." She said standing in front of him so he could tell she was completely naked under that

T-shirt with her fully erect nipples protruding through the T-shirt.

"Felicia, this is hard enough as it is." He said turning his head trying not to lust off of her.

"I can see that from here." She said eyeing the lump in the front of his slacks.

"I'm serious, I need to clear the air on this and then I have to go. I have people waiting on me." Ramon said turning back to face her.

"By people you mean Connie?" She said walking pass him to take a seat beside him.

"When you gone let her go and get with me and make it official." She said crossing her legs and facing him.

"It's not that simple. At first it was, but now things have changed." He said as he reached into his pocket and removed a cigar and a lighter.

"What do you mean...changed?" She said rolling her neck and smacking her lips.

"It's not that I don't appreciate everything you've done for us, but have a baby boy by my brother and..."

"Hold up Ramon!" She said putting a hand up and cutting him off. "That's not Thomas's son. That's Leonard's baby." She said before hanging her head down.

"What the fuck you mean that's not my nephew?" he said jumping off the sofa.

"Calm down Ramon. Let me explain." She said sticking the cigar in his mouth. He already knew she was a good liar now he wanted to see just how good.

"I'm 'bout to do something I never did in my life and to be totally honest with a man; well, since I first fell in love with Leonard. Ramon, I tried to trap Thomas because of the power associated with y'all family's name but Thomas care more about his alcohol than me or my son. I think he knows but he'd rather stay away from us and make our lives easier than to have to face the reality every day." She said crying silent tears as she poured her heart out.

"So you got my Mama and everybody believing a fucking lie! Damn lying to me but my Mama? Felicia that's some fucked up shit." He said blowing smoke in the air, thinking to himself this one sick bitch!

"Ramon, you got to understand where I was at in my life. You should know better than anyone else how cruel these streets are. I fucked and sucked to survive. I ain't waste my time fucking married men for $20 quickies, then have to hand that off to some fake ass wanna be pimp. Fuck that. I got bills and a standard of living to maintain. I saw Thomas as security," she said.

"Why is that?" he asked looking at her differently now.

"No offense, Thomas is a lame Ramon. You know it as well as I know it. Lames are security for females like me. Stank was a lame that was in the game so he had a purpose. I had to move up." She said point blank.

"So, I'm the next rung on your ladder of success." He said, as he sat back on the sofa.

"No Ramon, you are not the next rung, you're the last rung. I ain't never take money and buy a man nothing before besides Leonard, and his ass won't worth the nut that got him here fo 'real. But Ramon, you are power and strength. You're a man's man and a woman's dream. The things I did, was for you. All I ever wanted was for you to love me and treat me like I want to be treated. Is that so hard for you to understand?" She said dropping on her knees in front of him and placing her hands on his knees looking up at him.

"I understand that, but I can't trust you like I trust Connie." He said taking his hands and running it through her hair.

"Connie can't do for you what I can do and she won't do for you what I've done." She said looking into his eyes. In his heart, he wanted to believe her, but in his mind, he just couldn't.

"Okay Felicia, this is what I want you to do. I need for you to go get the duffle bag of money out the room for me."

Without hesitation, she sprung to her feet and ran to her son's room to get the bag and dropped it on the coffee table as soon as she returned. Ramon counted out two hundred stacks.

"Here," he said sliding the money over to her.

"I can't take that Ramon." She was shaking her head.

"Look, I got to go away on a business trip and this should hold you til I get back. I'll be in touch." He said getting up off the sofa.

"Now walk me to the door." He said grabbing the bag as he walked toward the door.

"You promise that this ain't over and we'll finish this at a later time?" she asked holding the door open for him.

"Yeah, my word is my bond," He said before he grabbed her and kissed her long and deep.

"Damn. Finally," she thought as she felt the sparks in her head burst and passion overcome her. The longer he kissed her, the more she felt the familiar explosion of her orgasm hit.

"Um, Um, Um, Um," She came hard and shook in his arms. That was all the assurance either needed to know that it was real.

Ramon helped her until she regained her senses.

"You good?" he asked.

"I'd be better if you could make me cum again." She said.

"Yeah, you good." He said releasing her.

"Turn around and let me see something." He said.

Felicia turned around and looked over her shoulder as Ramon lifted her T-Shirt up to see her pretty round ass.

"Like what you see?" She asked licking her lips.

"Hell yeah, I want you just like this when I come back from my business trip." He said, noticing nothing but the love juices running down her inner leg. As he turned to walk away, he smacked her on the ass.

"Oh!" She said.

"Now lock the door, I gotta go!"

As he turned and left, Felicia shut the door, took the stacks of money and dumped them on the floor, laid on top of them, and pleasured herself as she had orgasms over and over through the night thinking about Ramon.

When Ramon pulled up to his mother's house, it was about 8 o'clock at night. Soon as he walked through the door, Connie ran and jumped in his arms.

"Hey Boooo! I was so worried," she said sticking her tongue in his mouth before he could get a word out.

"Boy come on in here and shut the door." Sandra said getting up off the sofa. Connie let go of him long enough to sit the bag down and shut the door, then she went right back at it.

"Connie, let my baby go." Hattie Mae said coming from the kitchen.

"Come on and eat, the food is getting cold" she said coming towards her son and wiping her hands off in her apron. Ramon let Connie go and grabbed his favorite girl.

"Hey mama." He said before kissing her on the cheek.

"You know you don't have much time." She said

"I know is everyone here." He asked pulling the bag back up over his shoulder.

"Yeah, they're at the table." She said as he made his way into the kitchen, everyone was waiting on him and one by one they greeted him, and sat down at the table to enjoy a family dinner. This hadn't happened since their father had died and his empty chair brought back painful memories. Yet, he knew it would be the last time for a while that everyone will be together.

"I'm glad y'all came down, this won't be long because I'm on borrowed time as it is," Ramon sad as he finished his plate.

"Tousant you're doing well at Longwood and I want you to get your degree. So this should pay for it," Ramon said, pulling out 70 gee stacks and handing it over to him.

"Wow, thanks bruh, but what are you gonna do if you give me all of this?" Tousant asked. "Man, I'm straight, just promise me, you're gonna finish school and do better for us as a family." Ramon said.

"Without a doubt, bruh. I got you." Tousant said, as he accepted the money and gave his brother a hug.

"Okay, Sandra, you always running around here fixing people hair so this is for you to go to school and open up your own hair salon." He pulled out 50 stacks and handed it to her.

"Thomas you got a lot of issues bruh, I hope you find a way to deal with your inner demons. I'm not a saint; however, I've come to grip who I am and what I've become. Here." Ramon said handing him a piece of paper.

"What's this?" Thomas asked frowning his face. It's the address for a rehab center, check yourself in and when you come out, you'll be straight bruh." Ramon said showing deep concern.

"Man, I ain't got no problem. I drink here and there but it ain't no problem." Thomas said reaching for his glass of beer.

"If it ain't a problem put the glass down." Ramon challenged him.

"What?" he said grabbing his glass.

"Put the glass down and don't take another drink then." Ramon said to him.

"You don't take another drink, I'm grown and I got this under control. Just drop me something and go on with your little farewell address," He said.

"Thomas, I know you ain't talking to your brother like that." Hattie Mae said clearly upset.

"It's cool mama, just take this deed to the house over Highland Park on 4th avenue along with my car keys. When he gets it together, give it to him." Ramon said.

"Ray and Hank," he said turning his attention to them,

"Y'all got to go see Boo Boo and Ski Bo tomorrow. They got y'all covered." He said getting up from the table with the bag he walked over to his mama. "Mama, take the rest of this and let me get that thing," he said.

"Here you go baby." She said reaching into her bra and removing the paper. "Safest place on earth," she said smiling at him.

"Well you gone have to find another safe place because this won't fit." He said motioning towards the bag.

"Now where's my cake?" he asked going back to his seat at the table to finish his dessert.

"Dispatch to h-20, come in h-20." The voice said over the radio.

"This is h-20 over." Detective Hutch said sitting in his car parked up at Jefferson Village Apartments.

"I'll patch Sgt. Johnson through." The female dispatcher said.

"Yo Hutch, you copy." Sgt. Johnson said.

"Yeah, I copy go head." He responded.

"My informant said the rooster is at his mama hen house right now. So meet at one-one as soon as you can." Sgt. Johnson said.

"I'm in route now, what's your 25." Hutch said starting his car.

"I'm just leaving out the station I'll meet you there, over and out." Sgt. Johnson said, as he got in the car.

"Copy that out," Hutch said as he backed out of the complex. When they met up on 11th street they saw Ramon's car parked outside of the house.

"Are you sure he's in there? Detective Hutch said, standing outside of the Johnson's car at the driver's side window.

"My sources are good, trust me." Johnson responded.

"Okay let's go." Detective Hutch said backing away from the driver's side door allowing him to get out of his car. They cocked their guns and headed straight to the house.

"Take the back." Hutch said to Johnson. Johnson ran to cover the back. Hutch watched the front door closely and turned his walkie-talkie off. He gave Johnson a minute to get in position and approached the front door.

"Boom boom boom. Police open up!" He said banging on the door before kicking it open and rushing in with his gun drawn. Sandra and Thomas hit the floor.

"Oh God! Don't shoot! Don't shoot!" Sandra cried, as she lay stretched out the floor, they heard the sound of the back door crashing open.

"Get down! Get down!" Sgt. Johnson said to Hattie Mae and Tousant; neither moved. "Get out of my house cracker!," Hattie Mae spat at him.

"Get on the ground now," Johnson screamed pointing his gun back and forth between Hattie and Tousant.

"Cracker get that gun out my mama face!" Tousant said feeling his anger rise.

"Anyone else in the house?" Detective Hutch asked Sandra and Thomas.

"No, ain't nobody else here. Don't let that cracker kill my mama man." Thomas said attempting to get up.

"Stay down, I got you. Just don't get up." Detective said, as he walked towards the kitchen.

"Everything alright in there?" Detective Hutch asked as he peeped around the corner. It was a standoff.

"Y'all crackers killed my husband, and Fat Man, now y'all want to kill my baby Ramon but that'll be over my dead body." She screamed while tears ran down her face.

"Cracker get that gun out of my mama face!" Tousant said lunging at Sgt. Johnson causing his weapon to discharge as they struggled for control over the gun, falling to the floor.

"Get off my baby." Hattie Mae said stepping forward and grabbing his arm.

"Get off my..." she said falling to one knee before lying flat on the floor.

"Mama!" Tousant said, as he broke Sgt. Johnson's hold on the gun and kicked it away. Tousant ran over to aid his mother.

"Sandra, Sandra," Tousant called from the kitchen,

"Come help mama." Sgt. Johnson managed to get his gun and point it at Tousant.

"Boom Boom!" Sgt. Johnson shot his gun in the air.

"Motherfucker are you crazy?" detective said to him.

"Look let go of her and get on the ground." Sgt. Johnson said half out of breath.

"I'm placing you under arrest for assaulting an officer of the law. Hutch, search the house for Ramon." Sgt. Johnson said reaching for his pair of handcuffs.

"I'm not going anywhere until you call help for my mother." Tousant said as Thomas entered the kitchen and pushed Det. Hutch to the side.

"Look, I'll call it in." Det. Hutch said picking up his radio.

"H-20 to dispatch." Hutch said into his radio after turning it back on.

"This is dispatch go head" the dispatcher said.

"I need medical assistance to 1200 12th street, code red. Copy that dispatch." he said.

"Dispatch copy EMS is in route. H-20 I was told to inform you that Ramon Baker Jr. has just been taken into custody, he turned himself in. copy." Dispatcher said.

"H-20 copy over and out." Detective Hutch looked at Sgt. Johnson and shook his head.

"All of this for nothing!" Hutch said placing his gun in his holster and walking out the kitchen.

"Arrest! I beat these things with my eyes closed. As soon as Det. Hutch gets here we'll work this out." He said opening up his brief case.

"Tap tap" officer Alston knocked on the door.

"You may enter." David said.

"Excuse me, but Mr. Woolworth may I see you for a moment." Officer Alston said peeping his head inside the door.

"Yes of course, please excuse me Ramon," he said getting up and leaving the room.

"Come here." Officer Alston said waving him out of Ramon's ear shot.

"What seems to be the problem?" he asked.

"Commander Hicks just called and informed me that Mrs. Hattie Mae Baker has just been hospitalized. No word on her condition but she seems to have suffered from an apparent heart attack." He said looking at David.

"My God, does it ever end for this family? Okay, we won't say anything until later on. Where's Detective Hutch?" he asked officer Alston.

"At the hospital waiting to hear her status," He answered.

"Waiting to know her status, why is he even there?" David wondered.

"Well he and another officer conducted an illegal search of her home looking your client, a struggle ensued and his mother had a heart attack." Officer Alston said looking towards the floor.

"What kind of circus are you people having running around here? I'll stall for time but get his ass down here." David said as he walked back into the interview room.

"Okay, where was I?" he said shutting the door.

"You were stroking your ego." Ramon said looking at him in disgust.

"Oh yea, as I was saying I got a way to get you a good deal if you want it?" he said ignoring Ramon's last comment.

"I don't want no deal with you or your people that got anything to do with this," he said to David, as he sat back in his chair.

"I'm sure Tank briefed you on the developments, but here's a short recap. He and Jane called me for legal advice; I found a solution to satisfy all parties involved. I talked it over with the judge and the Commonwealth's attorney. They both are willing to play ball. All you have to do is want to play," David said going back in his briefcase.

"I'll hear you out but the minute you say something crazy, you're fired." Ramon said sitting up in his chair. Okay Ramon, this is the deal. You plead guilty to accessory after the fact of two counts of murder. That's all they can give you because they don't have a witness to the actual shootings. However, they got a witness that has placed you on more than one murder scene. Nonetheless, you'll be sentenced to 24 months that's 2 years in prison without parole and you'll be banned from the state of Virginia for the rest of your life." David said.

"Banned from the state for life, how the fuck am I supposed to conduct business from another state?" Ramon asked searching for the logic in the deal.

"You can still conduct business, but you won't be hands on. I think it's better that way," David replied.

"Tap tap"

"Excuse me, is it alright for me to come in?" Det. Hutch said.

"Boy am I glad to see you, a moment outside please." David said getting up and ushering him outside the door.

"What the hell is wrong with you? Y'all almost cost us everything with that stunt." He was cut off by Det. Hutch

"Look man I feel bad enough I fucked up, so after tonight it's over I quit." He said looking at the floor.

"Don't be stupid, you know too much. So this is how you make it right. You're going to draw up new charges for accessory after the fact. That's it nothing more nothing less." David said.

"That's it and we good?" he asked David.

"Yeah, oh and don't say nothing about his mother. How is she anyway?" David asked him.

"She's stable, they said she'll make it," he answered, looking at David letting out a sigh of relief.

"Thank God. Let's get this over with." David said as he walked back into the interview room.

"Well Ramon, it's all taken care of, now if you'll just give me the list this matter will be concluded." David said as he extended his hand to Ramon.

"Mane you got to be crazy. When the deal is signed and sealed you'll get the pussy ass list. Until then it's gone stay where it's at." Ramon said as he leaned back in the chair.

"But my people want to be assured everything is in proper hands," David said still holding his hand out.

"Well if you can get the deal done tomorrow, that's when you'll get the list." He said,

"Tomorrow?" David asked.

"My word is my bond." Ramon said.

When he returned back to booking, he gave Deputy Bower the signal and he headed to the phone. Deputy Bower called Tank on the phone.

"Hello" Tank said.

"Number two is safe; He said he'll see you tomorrow." Deputy Bower said hanging up the phone and dialing another number.

"Hello" Ronnie said answering her phone.

"Tell the queen her king will be in court tomorrow." After he hung up the phone he walked by Ramon's holding cell.

"It's done." He said as he continued his rounds.

In the John Marshall court building, the next morning in Judge Robert Doby's courtroom, the bailiff called the case.

"The case of the Commonwealth of Virginia versus Ramon Baker Jr. is now in session; the honorable Judge Robert Doby presiding." She said,

"You may be seated," Judge Doby said taking his seat.

"Is the defendant present?" he asked

"He is and he's represented your honor," David said. "Let the record reflect that David Woolworth is defense counsel." Doby said.

"Is the Commonwealth ready to proceed?" Doby asked

"Yes, your honor," Commonwealth's Attorney Joe Morris said. "Does the defendant understand the charges brought against him?" Doby said.

"Yes sir your honor." David said.

"How does he plead?" Doby asked "guilty your honor may I approach." David said as he and Joe approached the bench. They spoke briefly and returned to their assigned stations.

"Mr. Baker we have a rare case of developments in which I've been informed that a plea agreement has been met, am I correct?" Doby asked.

"Yes sir." Ramon answered.

"Do you fully understand the terms of this plea and is it your own choice to plead guilty," Doby asked. "Yes," Ramon answered.

"Okay, well I accept your plea of guilty, do you gentlemen have a date to set formal sentencing?" Doby asked

"Your honor, it is in my client's wishes that you impose his sentence here today." David said.

"Are there any objections?" David asked Joe.

"No your honor, we'll like to dispose of this matter as soon as possible." Joe said.

"Okay, Mr. Baker if you'll sign the plea agreement I'll formally sentence you," Doby said, as David handed Ramon the paperwork. Ramon signed his signature and passed it back to David. David handed it to the bailiff to take to the judge. Doby quickly overlooked the paperwork and then signed off.

"Everything seems to be in order. Mr. Baker you plead guilty to two counts of accessory after the fact of murder. I sentence you to the maximum penalty of each count with the added condition that you serve your term without the possibility of parole and that upon your release you are banned from the Commonwealth of Virginia for the rest of your natural life. This court is adjourned." Doby said as he banged the gavel. Ramon reached in his pocket and gave David the list.

"You know I got a copy of this just in case," Ramon said

"You gave your word, Ramon." David said.

"Man, this it I don't care about the list. It served its purpose." Ramon said as the bailiff came to escort him out the courtroom. He turned to Ronnie and Connie and smiled and mouthed the words, "the king shall return..."

Chapter 16

When Ramon entered the bullpen he was greeted by a small crowd of unfamiliar faces. Most were awaiting court. The guys whom had ridden from the lockup with him were sent to different courtrooms. Ramon searched the crowded room and found a space in the corner of the room in the back near the door that leads to the elevator.

"How much time did you get?" an old man sitting beside him asked.

"Enough now leave me alone." Ramon said as he reached in his pocket and pulled out a pack of Newports. The old guy thought to himself,

"This dude done got hit with a big number. Bad as I want one of those cigarettes, I better not test this youngster."

"Name's Bob." The older man said.

"Nice to meet you Bob, but I didn't come here to make friends and I'm not up for a game of 20 questions right now.

So if you don't mind?" Ramon said, looking him in a way that's universally understood.

"My bad, I don't want no problems." Bob said, as he moved close to the door that leads to the courtroom. Ramon thought of how Fat Man got blamed for Det. Howard's murder and was only charged with removing the gun from the scene, and he was also charged for helping Fat Man dump Stank's body in a vacant apartment. Once again Fat Man saved his ass. Regrets of his past caused his thoughts to travel to his mother and Sandra. They'd be alright they have more than enough money to survive and last until I come home. Then there's Felicia. It's time to see if she can back up all that queen shit now. She got to put up or shut up. This is the ultimate test of dedication for both her and Connie. Connie has youth on her side, but hopefully she won't get caught up in the fold and let other females talk her off the ride with him. Ramon heard some keys jingle as the door that leads to the elevator opened up. "Baker, Ramon Baker Jr." the deputy said.

"That's me, Ramon replied dryly.

"Come on." The deputy said placing a set of handcuffs on Ramon's wrists.

"Okay Convict, you got 5mins." the Deputy said as pointed to the row of black rotary phones that set on the a wooden bench.

Ramon gave him the look of death as he walked pass him and quickly grabbed one of the phones.

"Hello!" Hank said as he answered the phone.

"What's up Lil Bro.?" Ramon replied with a hint of excitement in his voice.

Hank hesitated at the sound of his brother's voice.

"Damn what's the matter? I ain't call collect and if I did I can pay for my own calls." He said jokingly.

"Nah it ain't that brah. " Hank replied.

The tone in his voice quickly let Ramon know that something was wrong.

"What's going on brah?" Ramon asked in a tone that was all business.

"Mane it's Moma." Hank said reluctantly.

"What about Moma?" Ramon asked as he felt his blood pressure rise and sweat trickle down the back of his neck.

Hank let his mind race to find an easy way to say it but it was no easy way.

"She's in the hospital. "

"What the fuck!" Ramon yelled as he slammed the phone receiver against the wall smashing it in pieces and began to sob uncontrollably.

No Brakes Publishing Order Form

Title	Quantity	Price	Total
Boy I Had Enough		$15.00	
Southside King		$15.00	
Ratchet Ville – Vol 1-3		$15.00	
To Live and Die in LA		$15.00	
Natural Born Killaz		$15.00	
Girl I Had Enough		$15.00	

Shipping and Handling $5.60

Name _____

Address: _____

_____

City: _____ State: _____ Zip Code: _____

Email: _____

Mail order form along with money order for payment to:

No Brakes Publishing
Attn: Author Terry Wroten
7324 Crenshaw #10
Los Angeles, CA 90043

Also available from No Brakes Publishing

Natural Born Killaz

To Live & Die in LA

Girl, I Had Enough

Molly

Ratchet Ville

Ratchet Ville 2

Ratchet Ville 3

Corporate Thuggin'

Good Girl Gone Bad

Ghetto Diva

ANTHOLOGY

The Massacre

www.ingramcontent.com/pod-product-compliance
Lightning Source LLC
Chambersburg PA
CBHW070059260626
47160CB00004B/1258